# VIOLA PUMPERNICKEL

## *and the*

# EMERALD LADY

## BY JO BAXTER

First published in paperback in Great Britain 2018
Second edition 2019

Text copyright © Jo Baxter

Cameo illustration © Andy Catling

Cover design by Claire Elizabeth

Jo Baxter asserts the moral right to be identified as the author of the work

ISBN: 9781796362701

For Jennifer

xxx

# VIOLA PUMPERNICKEL

didn't look like your average heroine.

But then again, Viola Pumpernickel *wasn't* your

## AVERAGE HEROINE...

London, England.
Sometime in the 1800s.

# Chapter One
### The Bravest Girl in London

As the blaze ripped through the building, she stood watching the flames flickering wildly. The heat was almost unbearable. Loud crackling and hissing from within the shop sent a shiver down her spine. Watching from the street, the wall of fire was making her skin tingle, but she knew she had to help the old man trapped inside.

*BOOM!*

An explosion inside the shop forced her and her fellow by-standers back as the window shattered. Viola hit the floor with such force that all the air was sucked out of her tiny body. She lay for a second, struggling to breathe, struggling to move. Her ears felt peculiar - as if her head had been wrapped in wool - and the once roaring sound of the fire was now a distant bubble. Eventually, she found her feet and took in as many breaths as she could to feel better. After a moment or two, her senses seemed to wake up and the pandemonium around her became instantly loud and frantic. Her back screamed in agony from the fall but she had to get up.

Having lived on this street all her life, she knew the buildings well and she knew there would be a back door. Pushing through the crowd, who were also trying to recover from the blast, she ran down the winding, narrow street to the alley that ran behind the row of shops. Viola could see the thick plumes of grey-black smoke puffing from the upstairs windows.

She needed something to climb over the fence. It took her a few attempts but eventually, using a discarded wooden crate, she managed to scramble over and land on the other side, tearing the skirt of her dress as she did so. Thankfully, the fire hadn't reached the back door yet. She ran and banged on the glass, hoping the old man could hear her. She was desperate to save him, but with every passing second, her hopes sank.

*Maybe I'm too late.*

She stopped beating on the door as tears filled her eyes. She looked to the ground, deeply saddened; she had known Mr Jeffers all her life and was a frequent visitor to his book shop.

"Help me!" cried a weak voice from behind the door. She grabbed the handle and pulled at it desperately, but it wouldn't budge. Viola looked around for something to break the window, and seeing a large rock sitting a few feet away from her, she went to lift it. It was far heavier than she had expected, so she let out a moan of frustration. She took a step back as tears streamed down her face, the man's cries for help echoing through the building.

*I am not giving up.*

Using all her strength, she slowly lifted the rock and launched it at the glass, shattering it into a thousand tiny pieces. Through the fuzzy smoke that poured out, Viola could see Mr Jeffers staggering to the opening. Dazed and confused by what was happening around him, he frantically grabbed at the smashed window, cutting his hands on the remnants of broken glass.

"Stop!" Viola said, pulling open her coat. She ripped it from her body and lay it across the dangerous shards. "Now climb up!" Viola yelled, pointing to a table that sat beneath the window. Mr Jeffers obeyed and was soon hanging out of the window. Viola grabbed his shoulders and pulled him down to the ground. His breathing sounded shallow and bubbly. He struggled to find clean air as Viola rubbed his back.

"We need to move," Viola said, pulling Mr Jeffers to his feet as the crackling grew louder.

"You saved me. Thank you, my angel," he spluttered.

"I *had* to save you, Mr Jeffers," she smiled. "You need to tell me which book to read next."

Mr Jeffers laughed in response as red hot flames shot through the broken window.

Viola sat on a wall, a little way from the scene of the blast, watching the firemen put out the last of the fire. It was finally under control, having been burning for hours. She had been the one to initially raise the alarm, having smelt the burning whilst she was out running an errand for her father. She had seen smoke seeping from an upstairs window and cried out for help. A lad, who was busy trying to break a piece of wood against a wall, ran off to the fire station to get help. Viola's family owned a bakery in the same area, and they had become very good friends with Mr Jeffers over the years. His shop, Jeffers Books, was one of Viola's most favourite places to spend an afternoon, looking at all the wonderful books in peace and quiet.

"Excuse me, miss?" said a fireman appearing at her side.

"Yes, sir?" Viola replied, looking up at him. He was the tallest man she had ever seen and his face was covered in soot. He looked like he needed a warm bath and a good night's sleep.

"I understand you helped to get Mr Jeffers out? You'll be glad to know he's with the doctor and he should be just fine." Viola closed her eyes and smiled as relief washed over her. "Here, for your trouble. Treat yourself to a nice cream cake." He handed her a coin.

"Thank you, sir!" Viola beamed.

"What's your name, miss?"

"Viola Pumpernickel, sir," she replied proudly.

"Well, Viola Pumpernickel, you might just be the bravest girl in London."


"Read all about it, fire destroys shop in Brookwater Lane. Old man pulled from blaze! Read all about it! Old man survives fire!" cried a lad selling newspapers from a cart, the following day. Viola ran to the boy and asked for a copy. He rolled his eyes but agreed to let her look at one – just so long as she gave it right back to him. He couldn't go around giving them away for free, after all.

Viola opened the paper and slowly read the article. Her reading wasn't quite as good as yours or mine, but she could just about get by:

```
"A fire ripped through a shop in Brookwater
Lane yesterday, trapping an old boy, Jeremy
Jeffers, within its burning walls. Thanks to
the unyielding efforts of our mighty Fire
Engine Establishment, he was pulled to safety
and is now recovering well. The same cannot be
said for his shop which, by all accounts, is a
charred shell of its former self."
```

Viola's shoulders dropped.

"They didn't mention me," she whispered.

"Well, why would they? You're just a girl," the lad said, snatching the paper back. He pushed his cart away from her, yelling the headlines again.

Viola clenched her jaw in anger. In that moment, she promised herself she would show the people of London just how powerful this girl could be.

The doctors called Viola 'slight' for her twelve years which meant that people treated her as if she were made of china. Although she was a lovely little thing with wavy, straw-coloured hair and the biggest blue eyes you were ever likely to see, Viola wasn't a particularly girly-girl. She much preferred making mud pies with her brothers than playing with dollies or hopscotch with her friends, thank you very much.

Viola would often sit on the step to her father's bakery watching the world go by, spending hours imagining the lives the strangers led that passed through the cobbled streets of London. Her father, Albert Pumpernickel, was famous throughout the whole of the city for selling the tastiest bread, his speciality being sultana and banana loaf. Mary Pumpernickel, Viola's mother, grew fresh fruit and vegetables in their small courtyard behind the shop and often traded her pickings for raisins and bananas from old Mr Granger at the grocers so that Albert could make his much loved, delicious loaf.

Although the Pumpernickels were famous in London for their scrumptious bread, they weren't a wealthy family and would often rely on leftovers from the bakery or tradings with the butcher to provide their dinner. Thankfully, Viola's mother was a wonderful cook and could somehow make even the blandest of foods taste really rather yummy.

Despite being a little poor, they were a happy bunch who loved each other very dearly. As well as Viola, there were two other children of the family - her younger brother Rupert, who was eight years old, and her older brother Edward who had just turned fifteen.

Young Rupert was a gentle soul and he loved his siblings but would often turn down their invitations to play with them, instead playing on his own with his wooden toy soldiers. Like Viola, he was rather small and his clothes would normally fit children a few years younger than him. He had been a very poorly baby and was often seen by the local physician, Dr Anderson. When he was sick, every new day would bring visitors from all over the town, mostly friends of Albert and Mary, who would bring gifts of food and clothing for Rupert, and they would spend hours sitting with Mr and Mrs Pumpernickel, talking closely and quietly. Rupert, thankfully, got much better and the visits gradually stopped.

Rupert, however, never ever spoke. His parents had tried to coax him into saying "hello" or "goodbye", "mama" or "papa", but he just didn't seem interested. Mary used to cry a lot, thinking that her son was unhappy, but the doctor assured her that Rupert would speak when he was ready. Viola found that she could communicate quite well with her little brother and, more often than not, she would know what he meant without him having to actually use any words.

On the other hand, Edward, or 'Teddy', the oldest Pumpernickel child, was a very confident lad. He was tall and broad with mousy brown hair. He was so tall in fact, that he had to wear their father's clothes which, according to their mother, made Teddy look like a "proper grown up." Teddy was bright and outgoing and often worked with their father in the shop. Their father regularly told them that when he was too old and tired to run the shop, Teddy would take it over, something that he was very excited to do, as and when the time came.

Teddy was far more serious about life than Viola. Every day he would arrange the bread in the shop window to attract passing trade, and he'd constantly sweep the floors of flour and filth to keep the shop looking clean and tidy. He was also fiercely protective of

Viola and Rupert and made sure that any bullies were put strictly in their place. No one would ever hurt them whilst Teddy was around.

Mrs Pumpernickel often called Viola fanciful - a daydreamer, a fantasist, and would try to encourage her to help in the bakery or with her in the home, rather than sitting outside all alone. She believed that Viola should know how to sew and how to cook so that when she was married with children, she would be able to run a happy home. Viola, however, had other ideas on how best to spend her time. She liked people watching and enjoyed creating her own little world filled with mysteries and excitement. Cooking and cleaning could wait.

Of course, being a fanciful child meant that not a lot of grown-ups would believe her when she told them about all the weird and wonderful things she saw in the streets of London. For example, no one believed her when she told them about the "Man with the Silver Cane" who she was convinced was a wicked old headmaster. He was tall and spindly with a thin, grey moustache and deep-set, brown eyes. He always wore a top hat and often checked his pocket watch for the time. He looked different from most of the other residents of Brookwater Lane; his clothes weren't torn or threadbare, his shoes weren't full of holes or two sizes too tight. In fact, he always looked very smart indeed. Every now and again, however, he would scowl at Viola as he passed, peering over his thin rimmed, metal glasses at her. He never visited the bakery but seemed to glare in whenever he passed. He had a stern look about him and Viola often imagined him barking orders at the poor little children, making them tremble with fear as they heard the *tap, tap, tap* of his cane on the cold hard school floors approaching them.

Another character that grabbed Viola's attention was "The Purple Pickpocket." He was a small, unkempt lad who always wore the same clothes; a tatty purple waistcoat over a grubby white shirt with a dark green tie. His grey trousers were dirty and housed several tears and frays. He wore a thin, grey cap over his shaggy brown hair that was even longer than Viola's. Viola guessed he was probably around fifteen-years old - he looked the same age as Teddy. Every day he would stand in the lane outside the bakery and watch the public go about their lives, just like Viola did. However, he seemed to be rather clumsy as he would often bump into people very suddenly, but he was always very polite, apologising for his awkward behaviour. He would then laugh to himself and swiftly disappear into one of the many alleyways. He really was quite peculiar. Viola's father called the young lad a pickpocket, which, Viola was shocked to discover, meant that he stole wallets and jewellery from passers-by without them even knowing. Viola and her brothers knew it was terrible behaviour and something that was wholly wrong. However, Viola always felt a little sad for the Purple Pickpocket.

There were lots of characters in her stories that Viola knew the real names of, of course. There was Constable Adam Clancy, the local policeman, Dr Clyde Anderson and Father Jack Kelly, to name just three. They were all known to the community and were all perfectly friendly. Father Kelly would often ruffle her hair as he left the bakery, a loaf of bread nestled under his arm, and he would ask God to bless her as he did so.

Constable Clancy would perform magic tricks to entertain the local children, and it worked every time. Not with Viola, of course. Ever since she could talk, she would claim that magic wasn't real. She would watch children react with shock and awe at the policeman retrieving a penny from behind their ears, knowing that he simply hid the coin in his hand and showed it at the last minute. She also worked out very quickly how he would bend a spoon or how he made a pencil float in the air. Although she didn't believe in magic, she was always intrigued by how a trick was created. If she couldn't work it out immediately, it would play on her mind until she did. The children always seemed to enjoy watching these magic tricks so Viola kept up the act that only Constable Clancy could unlock the mysterious secret banks that lived behind their ears.

"I wish you would stop making up so many stories, Viola," her mother tutted one day, when Viola told her another tale, this time about a new character - The Raven Dog Catcher. Viola was convinced that he stole dogs from the street, usually strays, and sold them on the other side of London Bridge...or worse.

"I saw him again today. I don't like him, Mother. He seems very unkind," Viola said as she picked at a tiny hole in her apron. Mrs Pumpernickel was standing by the stove chopping some beef for dinner. Her father must have sold a lot of bread this week as they never had fresh meat unless he had done very well, or it was Christmas time, when he would trade loaves of cinnamon bread for a chicken from Bill Barnaby, the butcher.

They'd had similar conversations to this on numerous occasions; Viola had told her mother about Mrs Lovett the pie maker, who Viola claimed was selling pastries filled with human meat at her pie shop in Bell Yard. Viola said that she had seen Mrs Lovett, along with Mr Todd, the barber, dragging a huge sack filled with something big and heavy into Mrs Lovett's shop late one evening. Of course, nobody liked that particular story and despite Mrs Pumpernickel's protests, Viola was adamant that it was true. She had even heard a man say to a friend that he knew someone who went for a shave and never returned. Mr Todd denied that he had ever seen the man, despite his coat hanging on the hook in his shop. A frightening mystery, I think you'll agree.

"Please Viola, I will not have you speaking ill of strangers. Spreading such absurd rumours can be very damaging to those poor people. Now, pass me the spuds," her mother said, wiping her greasy hands on her apron before sliding the chopped beef into a saucepan with a knife. The mixture hissed and sizzled as the meat hit it, filling the room with a warm, inviting smell. Viola picked up the sack of potatoes that sat on the floor by the door and let out a moan of frustration as the sack split and a seemingly endless cascade of potatoes bounced off the floor. Viola looked up at her mother as they both began to giggle.

"Rupert!" Mrs Pumpernickel called out, hoping her youngest child was within earshot. He slowly appeared in the doorway, hoping he wouldn't be called away from his toys for too long.

"Help your sister with the spuds," Mrs Pumpernickel smiled, as she wiped the knife on a rag. Rupert sighed and gently put a toy soldier on the table before crouching to help Viola gather the potatoes. Rupert looked at Viola who smiled at him, thankful for his help. Viola handed a spud to her mother who asked for one more.

Already bored by the tedium of being in the kitchen, and having picked up the last potato, Rupert retrieved his soldier and held it to his chest. Mrs Pumpernickel nodded and silently waved him into the front room, signalling that he could return to his game.

"Can I go and play too?" Viola asked, hoping she could copy her brother's desire not to have to help cook the entire meal. Mrs Pumpernickel looked down at her daughter.

"You should learn how to cook, Viola. You should know how to sew a dress or a hem on a trouser leg. You'll be married one day and your husband won't know these things, I can tell you. It's expected of us womenfolk to know how to run a house."

"*Why* won't my husband cook and clean?" Viola said with a raised eyebrow. Mrs Pumpernickel laughed, a little too hard for Viola's liking.

"That's not the way things are, I'm afraid. Maybe one day you will change that," she smiled.

Viola rolled her eyes and let out a sigh. After a second, Mary put the knife down and crouched so that they were the same height. Although she was a lot bigger and twenty whole years older, her nose was the same as Viola's and her big blue eyes always gave away that they were mother and daughter.

"My love, promise me, no more make-believe." She spoke gently and pushed a stray hair behind Viola's ear.

"It's not make-believe, Mama-" Viola started. Mary placed a finger to her mouth.

"Promise me," she repeated. Viola nodded, being pulled into a hug by her mother. She was so frustrated that her mother never believed her but she knew it was pointless arguing. As she rested her head on her mother's shoulder, a bird flew in and sat on the window sill. Viola watched as he turned to her and winked.

"No more make-believe," Viola smiled.

## Chapter Two
*Thieves, Pickpockets and Whizzers*

Mr Pumpernickel had asked Viola to help Teddy create a wonderful window display to entice passing trade to come into the bakery and, having felt she had done a worthy job, she was now gazing at the passers-by who were slowly filling the streets, totally oblivious to her older brother quietly rearranging the display to make it a little more appealing to the customers. She sat on the step, swinging her grandfather's old pocket watch back and forth, something which she did without realising. It hadn't worked for as long as Viola could remember, but she somehow felt safer with it in her hands. It was almost like holding it close made her forget that her grandfather wasn't there anymore.

Mrs Pumpernickel's father, Edmund Beattie, died almost five years earlier. He had been a very fit and healthy man, but had developed pneumonia after jumping into the ice-cold River Thames to save a woman from drowning. Legend had it that Mr Beattie had been walking along the embankment when he saw the young woman struggling in the water. She was too far away for him to reach so he jumped in and dragged her to safety. She had swallowed a lot of water but was deemed to be healthy after a week or so in hospital. Mr Beattie, on the other hand, being twenty years older than the lady and his body unable to take being in the freezing water, succumbed to the sickness a few days later. Edmund Beattie was considered a hero for his valiant rescue and that made Viola simply burst with pride.

Viola adored her grandfather. He would often sit with her and tell her fantastic stories about the adventures he had when he was a boy as well as tales from his army days. Her parents believed Viola inherited her love of storytelling from him. Everyone in the town knew Edmund and they were all as fond of him as Viola was. If she thought about her grandfather too hard, she would get rather upset so she chose to only think about him for a moment at a time.

Viola sighed as she looked up from the watch. As usual, the poultry-hawkers had chickens running about the street outside the bakery all day, clucking and flapping their wings. Viola used to give the chickens names but she soon gave up as they never seemed to stay around long enough to learn them.

"Good morning, Miss Pumpernickel," Constable Clancy smiled as he walked past the shop, tipping his cap as he went. Viola waved back and chirped a greeting in response. He wasn't calling in for his bread today, so the trick that Viola had created in a bid to impress him would have to wait. As she watched him walk away from the shop, greeting his passers-by in a similar manner to Viola, her gaze moved to the alleyway on the other side of the street.

Cobble Lane was nestled between Barnaby's Butchers and a haberdashery that sold beautiful ribbons and thread which her mother sometimes purchased to make cloaks and what-not for Viola. Mrs Pumpernickel often said that she could happily spend all her time in there, looking at the lovely fabrics and fine silks. If she were a wealthy woman, she said, all three children would be dressed in the finest clothes and shoes, rather than the threadbare hand-me-downs and makeshift garments they currently wore.

Through the murky shadows, Viola saw a small, plump lady emerge from the alley. Her long, dark dress looked slightly grubby and covered a pair of muddy, well-used boots. An emerald shawl, peppered with tiny golden bells that jangled as she walked, sat on her rather broad shoulders. Her wild hair was as orange as a pumpkin and her face was round and pink. She glanced in both directions having left the alley and decided to walk left towards the docklands. As she turned, Viola saw she was carrying a large, multi-coloured handbag over her right arm, its contents bulging. The lady made her way down the street into the crowd before stopping suddenly. She turned slowly, her eyes finding Viola's. For a few seconds, their gaze was locked. Viola suddenly forgot how to breathe and she wasn't sure why.

Before Viola had a chance to stand, the lady had swiftly made her way through the people to the bakery and crouched down in front of her, their noses almost touching. She detected a feint whiff of lavender which was a surprising scent to find on such a fearsome woman.

"It's rude to stare, little 'un," she snarled, revealing a set of brown and yellow teeth, all spaced out and crooked. Viola nodded with a gulp. Her voice was trapped inside her throat. The lady glared at Viola for just a few seconds more before she stood up, straightening her dress. She dug her hands into her pocket and pulled out a purple spray of wild flowers tied together with twine. She handed it to Viola with a nod.

"W-wh-what is this?" Viola stuttered, taking the floret.

"Heather. It's for luck," she smiled. "Keep it safe." Viola nodded again, still afraid of the mysterious woman standing above her. "Now, you be careful of the maltoolers, won't ya?" She pointed to the pocket watch.

"The mal-who?" Viola asked, unfamiliar with the lady's choice of word.

"Thieves, pickpockets, whizzers...the nasty little crooks who'll rob you as soon as look at 'ya," the woman replied, as she pulled her emerald shawl tightly across her chest. Viola nodded, as the lady turned and headed off without saying another word. Viola watched her disappear into the crowd and looked down at the posy in her hand. She breathed in the subtle, earthy aroma and placed the flowers in her pocket. If it was a lucky charm, she needed to keep it close.

Viola was used to meeting peculiar characters in London. In fact, sometimes there were more peculiar people than not, so Viola hadn't given the Emerald Lady much thought in the passing days.

However, that all changed when her mother called her into the kitchen one afternoon. Viola had decided to stay at home, which consisted of a few small rooms above the bakery, as it was a particularly cold and rainy day and she'd rather play toy soldiers with Rupert than sit outside on her own. Teddy was helping in the shop so Viola knew her father didn't need her today, for which she was thankful. The shop was chilly at the best of times, let alone when it was so wintery outside.

"Where did you get this?" Mrs Pumpernickel asked when she finally made her way into the kitchen. She was holding one of Viola's dresses in one hand and the heather in the other.

"The Emerald Lady gave it to me," Viola answered, taking the spray out of her mother's hand. "It is lucky heather. She told me I must keep it safe." Viola pulled a face, realising she had failed in her duty.

"Who's the Emerald Lady?" her mother asked, feeling rather concerned. Viola explained that she was a woman who appeared out of the shadows, warning her of the dangers that the London streets offered.

"Her teeth were all brown and crooked!" Viola giggled. "And her green shawl jingled like Christmas sleigh bells."

Mrs Pumpernickel shook her head and threw the dress into the bucket she was using to wash a pair of her father's work aprons.

"What have I told you about your make-believe stories?" Mrs Pumpernickel said without looking at her. Her voice was sharp and loud.

"It is not make-believe, Mama. She's real," Viola frowned. Mrs Pumpernickel sighed but said nothing. "She told me about the whizzers and maltoolers." She suddenly remembered the strange words the Emerald Lady had used.

"This woman sounds rather dangerous. Promise me you'll stay away from her in future," Mrs Pumpernickel said, turning to face her daughter.

"Yes, Mama." Viola whispered.

"Go and play with your brother," she said almost in a whisper.

Viola turned and left the kitchen, clutching the floret of heather. Her mother had no cause for concern; she was far too scared of the Emerald Lady to ever speak to her again.

"Ladies and Gentlemen, for one night only, feast your eyes on the tremendously talented, the graciously gifted, the wonderfully wonderful - Miss Ruby and Mr Smith!" boomed a little man waving a handful of leaflets in the air. Together with Teddy and Rupert, Viola was playing a game of Hide and Seek in one of the many streets that splintered off Brookwater Lane.

Having found her younger brother's hiding spot behind a disused beer barrel, Viola and Rupert had made their way to Wilton's Music Hall, a small but popular theatre in Whitechapel. The man ignored the pair and continued to shout to the crowds. Viola picked up a flyer that was lying on the flagged street, instantly taken in by the image.

Rupert touched the flyer in her hand, pointing to a picture of a beautiful woman dressed in a long, stunning gown. She was tall and slim and, except for her mother, was the most beautiful woman Viola had ever seen.

"Miss Ruby," Viola read aloud. "She must be a very good dancer, Rupe. Look how many people want to see her." Viola pointed to the ever-growing line of people queuing to get one of the flyers from the man. Rupert's eyes widened as he nodded in agreement.

"For just tuppence, you can witness the spellbinding Miss Ruby and Mr Smith as they bring you the Waltz, the Gallop and fresh from Bohemia, the Polka!" the man continued, followed by 'oohs' and 'aahs' from his audience. Viola sighed. She loved dancing but knew that she wouldn't be allowed to go along. Children weren't permitted in places like this. The audience would drink a lot of alcohol and often get rather rowdy. Viola's father had been to a few shows and had sworn he would never go there again, saying it was full of 'reprobates and scoundrels.' She looked back at the picture in her hands and imagined what it must be like to glide across the stage, dancing to such lively and fun music.

Rupert pulled on Viola's hand, snapping her out of her daydream. Realising that her older brother was still hiding somewhere, Viola folded up the paper and stuffed it into the pocket of her apron. Her dream of dancing at the Music Hall would have to wait - she had a game of Hide and Seek to win.

They had been searching for Teddy for what felt like days. Rupert had led them down an alley that ran behind the theatre and smiled as he lifted a grubby old sack off a wooden crate, convinced he had found Teddy. The box was empty, however, save for a few oily rags. Viola sighed. She was getting tired and her tummy was rumbling. Rupert slumped on the crate and frowned. About to tell him they would have to admit defeat. Viola was distracted by a small grey dog that was chewing on something in the corner.

"Look," Viola whispered, pointing at the pooch. She slowly made her way over to him as Rupert stood shaking his head.

Viola touched her little brother gently on the arm to assure him she was fine and reached out to the dog, hoping he was as friendly as he looked. As she got closer to him, she saw that his back leg was badly cut and covered in dried blood and dirt. The poor thing was frantically licking and nibbling at the injury which looked dreadfully sore. A deep growl emanated from within the dog as he showed his sharp, yellow teeth. Viola jumped back, frightened by the sinister noise. She returned to her little brother who wrapped his tiny fingers around hers.

"Come on, Rupe. Let's go home," Viola whispered, squeezing his hand. She too was scared but didn't want to show her fear. The dog stopped growling but was staring at the pair with his big, brown eyes. He looked sad, but Viola knew not to try and touch him again. One warning was enough.

As Viola and Rupert went to leave the alleyway, they heard a whimper behind them. Viola turned to see a tall, thin man dressed in dark, tatty clothes throw a huge brown sack over the dog.

"The Raven Dog Catcher!" Viola gasped, her skin prickling with fear.

"Come 'ere you little-" he said as he struggled to scoop up the dog-filled sack.

"No!" Viola cried out. "Leave him alone!"

The man turned to her, his face hidden by the hood of his coat.

"I said, leave him alone," Viola repeated, her voice stronger this time. The man shuffled closer to her, still gripping the sack. For the first time, Viola saw his face. It was sunken and grey. His nose looked like it had been broken several times and was rather out of shape. She gasped at his shocking appearance.

"Go home, little girl," he growled, revealing black, pointed teeth. His hands were scarred and red and Viola saw that he was missing two fingers on his left hand.

"He's hurt his leg, he needs help," she cried, moving towards him. Although she was utterly terrified of the man, she couldn't let him take the dog away. She knew that he was stealing dogs – she *knew* she wasn't making it up.

"Out of my way," he sneered. Viola's heart was beating through her chest.

"Not until you set him free," she hissed, clenching her fist. "I mean it."

Rupert tried to pull her back, but Viola was determined to stand up to this man. She loved all animals and hated it when people were cruel to them.

The man started to laugh, quietly at first but it soon developed into a loud, booming laugh. He suddenly launched himself towards the Pumpernickels.

"Go home, you little ragamuffins. These streets ain't safe...nasty people roaming," he snarled. He smelt strongly of rum which made Viola feel most uncomfortable but she had to act quickly – if she didn't help this poor little pooch, nobody would. She kicked out her leg, whacking the man's shin with her big boots. As he recoiled in pain, grabbing his leg, the sack fell to the floor. Viola pulled at the opening, revealing the furry bundle inside. The man grabbed at the bag but Viola was too quick for him.

"Go! Run!" Viola pushed the dog out of the bag. He growled as she touched him but, realising she was there to save him, he escaped from the canvas prison and limped away into the shadows.

"You idiot girl!" the man roared, slowly standing up. "Do you know what you've just done?"

Terrified, Viola grabbed Rupert's arm and ran out of the alley, the sound of the man behind chasing them. He was getting closer and closer, crying out that they were in deep trouble. Desperately trying to escape the man, she wasn't paying attention to where she was going and crashed into a figure making his way into the snicket. The impact made her fall to the ground with a thud.

"Viola?" the voice asked.

"Teddy!" she cried, looking up at her brother. "You have to help us! We saved the dog but the Catcher is after us!" she said turning back to the alleyway. Teddy frowned, confused by her ramblings and helped her to her feet. Rupert pulled Teddy close, hugging his brother's leg.

"Calm down," Teddy said soothingly.

"The Catcher, he's after us," she said breathlessly. Teddy turned to look down the alley. The man, however, had disappeared.

"Don't worry, you're safe now," Teddy said, hugging his siblings tightly.

"He was hurting the dog. You do believe me, don't you, Teddy?"

"You're my sister, Viola. I will *always* believe you," he said, stroking her head.

# Chapter Three
## *A Thief in the Night*

Brookwater Lane was quiet and still. The thief had waited until the dead of night before he made his move. The landlord of the White Bear pub had locked up and finally gone to his bed, meaning that all the businesses were now closed for the night.

The thief quickly made his way to the watchmakers and, checking for a final time that he was alone, launched his elbow through the door window. As glass cascaded to the ground, he shoved his arm through the window and found the lock inside. He winced as he caught his jacket sleeve on the broken glass. Tugging his arm free, he twisted the door handle and was in. Just under ten seconds - not his quickest time but certainly not his worst.

The shop was dark, not unusual for this time of night, and a mixture of wood and metal aroma filled the air. He had decided not to bring his lamp in case someone spotted the light from outside. However, without it he couldn't see where he was going and kept hitting his knees on the various tables and cabinets within the shop. Becoming increasingly frustrated with bashing his legs, he reached into his pocket and pulled out a matchbook. As he lit a match, a huge smile spread across his face as he saw for the first time just what lay before him: gold pocket watches; carriage clocks; the finest jewellery - everything that was either being sold or fixed by Mr Fletcher. It was an absolute treasure-trove. Taking a chance, he lit a nearby lamp with his match and opened the sack he held under his arm, scooping up handfuls upon handfuls of the swag. It was better than he could ever have imagined. Cabinets stood along all the walls, full of trinkets and charms. Saving time, he used his trusty elbow to smash through the glass panels, grabbing everything he could from inside.

A noise from outside made him spin round. He froze as he watched a young couple walk by the shop, too busy chatting to each other to notice what was going on. He let out a sigh of relief and continued raiding the shop. He had to be quick – he had been told umpteen times not to hang around in there longer than was necessary.

*Get in, get the loot and get out.*

Happy that he had grabbed everything he could, he threw the sack over his shoulder and pushed his way back through the front door. As he stood in the street, he sniggered quietly to himself. He was getting better with every robbery. Surely his boss would realise his potential now? It was only a matter of time before he included him in his plans for "the big job" he kept talking about.

*Any day now...*

He took in a lungful of the night air and put his bag on the floor. He reached into his pocket and pulled out the matchbook again. This time, however, he also pulled out an old rag. He calmly lit a match and held the rag above it until the rag was engulfed with fire. He threw the rag into the shop and dropped the match to the floor, extinguished immediately by the puddle water.

He smiled as he watched the flames begin to flicker inside the shop and picked up his bag. The crackling and hissing from inside the building was getting louder and louder, which meant, of course, the fire was growing. As much as he wanted to stay and watch, he had to leave. He couldn't get caught with all the loot. Besides, he was eager to get home and have a proper look at what he had stolen.

A noise rang out from the other side of Brookwater Lane. He peered a little closer, but being so dark he couldn't see anything. A little concerned, he adjusted the sack on his shoulder and swiftly made his way back down Cobble Lane.

In the shadows, Viola stood frozen at the bottom of the bakery steps, having seen the whole thing.

The following morning, Brookwater Lane was bursting with police. The watchmakers, JD Fletchers, was surrounded by an ever-growing crowd of people, interested in seeing the state of the shop following the blaze. Albert, Mary and the children watched the commotion from within the bakery, as Constable Clancy made his way in.

"They have done considerable damage, I'm afraid. Stolen

everything that wasn't nailed down and trashed the rest before setting the place on fire. Utterly senseless," Constable Clancy said removing his hat. "It's a good job that Viola raised the alarm when she did. I understand you saw our villain, Viola?"

"Yes, sir. It was rather dark, but I know I would recognise him anywhere. I'm was a little frightened at first, but once I realised what was happening, I raced upstairs and told Papa and he went to the station to get you."

"Well, aren't you a clever girl," Clancy smiled, impressed at her actions.

"She certainly is," Mr Pumpernickel said gently, stroking his daughter's hair.

"Could you tell me what this thief looked like, Viola?"

"Short, about Father's height perhaps and round. In fact, he looked a little like a frog," she said, thinking about it. "But he wore a dark jacket, like a sailor, and tatty black trousers. Frogs don't wear clothes, of course."

Constable Clancy chuckled as he scribbled down on his notepad and put it back in his pocket.

"Thank you, Viola. You have been most helpful."

"Constable Clancy? Do you think that this man was the one responsible for the fire at Jeffers Books?" Mary asked, concerned.

"That is my concern, yes. They all seem to share a pattern. We may well be dealing with a serial thief and arsonist," he sighed. Mary shook her head and frowned. What sort of person could do this?

He said his goodbyes to the Pumpernickels and returned to the scene, speaking to the locals who were firing questions at him about the crime. Mary told her family to go upstairs and she would prepare them some breakfast. Albert declined and announced he was going to open the shop as normal – *the show must go on*, as he often claimed.

Viola stood in the street watching the commotion in front of her, wondering who could commit such a wicked crime. Granted, she never really liked Mr Fletcher, she thought he was a most peculiar man, but he didn't deserve to have his livelihood destroyed in such a violent way. Nobody did.

As she watched the crowd grow larger still with the police activity, Viola made her way over. Clancy was busy speaking with a newspaper reporter who no doubt would be eager to plaster the story over tomorrow's front page, so Viola was able to sneak a little closer to the shop undetected.

It was absolute chaos. The window had been smashed and glass lay everywhere. The once pristine shop was now a scene of carnage: broken clocks; shattered cabinets and tables; glass stands that once housed beautiful jewellery and the finest watches now lay decimated in the centre of the shop, half of which was charred by the fire.

Looking down to the ground, Viola spotted a large gold button lying amongst the shattered glass and burnt remnants. She bent down and picked it up, rubbing soot from it on her apron. She closely studied the intricate and beautiful pattern on the top; an anchor in the centre of the button with a beautiful crown resting on its head.

"Constable Clancy?" Viola called, standing up. He glanced over at Viola and frowned.

"You shouldn't be here, Viola. Go back home," he said gently.

"Look," Viola said, holding out her hand to show him the button.

"That's very interesting but I'm rather busy at the moment. Run along home and you can show me later," he said, patting on her the head.

"I found it here, Mr Clancy, in the shop. It could be the burglar's...he was wearing a naval jacket, wasn't he?"

He glanced at it for a second more, before raising an eyebrow. He took it from Viola and studied it closely. He put the button in his jacket pocket and smiled.

"Well spotted, Miss Pumpernickel," he whispered. "Well spotted indeed."

A few days later, Viola had taken her usual spot outside the bakery, perched on the bottom step. The air was dewy and fresh, having just recovered from a particularly nasty rain storm the night before. Viola liked the rain – it made the cobbled streets glisten and sparkle as the morning sun beamed down.

Watching a chubby, ginger cat drink from a puddle, Viola could hear her father chatting to a regular customer, Augustus Collicott. He was a very well-spoken, well-dressed man whose clothes were truly beautiful and obviously cost far more than Viola could ever imagine. They weren't torn or dirty or two sizes too small. He really was very dapper, as her mother often said.

"I don't know what to say, Albert," Mr Collicott said, jangling a few coins in his hands. As a well-respected solicitor in Whitechapel, his opinion was highly regarded and when he spoke, people listened. "You must be vigilant. These criminals will steal anything and everything unless you keep your eyes on them! You don't want to be next, do you?"

Mr Pumpernickel shook his head as he kneaded some dough for his next batch of bread.

"Some scoundrel stole my wheelbarrow last week! I know it's not the same as what poor Fletcher or Jeffers are going through but how on earth will I manage all of my deliveries now?" Mr Pumpernickel said with a frown. "With my back, I can't carry all the flour from the mill without my barrow. Who on earth pinches a wheelbarrow? It's older than dirt, not worth ha'pence." Mr Pumpernickel slammed his fist into the dough causing a huge puff of white flour to bellow into the air.

"Believe me, I have asked myself that very question."

"And why set fire to the shops, just for the sake of it? Coward," Albert sighed. Mr Collicott frowned and nodded.

"Reckless and foolish," Mr Collicott tutted, shaking his head. "Perhaps you should set up a contribution pot for them? Ask the locals to help them get back on their feet. This should get you started," he smiled, handing Albert a pound coin.

"Why, thank you, sir. What a wonderful idea," Albert beamed.

As the men said their goodbyes, the cat, who by now had finished drinking the puddle water, had scurried over to Viola. It stopped by her booted feet and looked up at her, curiously. As Mr Collicott left the shop, the cat turned and hissed at him, his hackles standing on end.

"Get away," Mr Collicott snarled, as the cat hid behind Viola's feet. "Vicious creature," he said, glaring at the little fella.

"Don't be so mean, sir. He won't hurt you, he's just curious," Viola said gently. Mr Collicott raised an eyebrow.

"Curiosity killed the cat, girl. You remember that," he said as he walked away, wholly unimpressed by the cat's presence. Rolling her eyes, Viola waved a goodbye. Although she had only just met this little cat, she felt instantly very defensive of him.

"Hello, little one," Viola said, not sure whether to touch the cat or not. Her parents had always told her to be wary of the local strays as they could be covered in fleas and mange and would, most likely, try to bite her. However, this little one looked well cared for and really rather kind. He wasn't a stray, she told herself. He couldn't be.

Viola reached out and gently touched his head. He let out a loud purr and threw himself onto the ground, exposing a thick, furry belly. Viola smiled and gently rubbed his tummy, making his purrs even louder. His fur was warm and velvety to the touch, and Viola was tempted to scoop him up for a cuddle. Remembering her mother's words of warning, however, she decided against it. As much as she loved animals, she didn't fancy having fleas.

"What's your name?" she asked, noticing he had a green collar around his neck. She pulled the collar round to find a little bell and a golden tag with a name scrawled across it.

"Hello, Walpole," she cooed, returning to stroke his belly. "You are a very handsome boy."

Suddenly, a loud bang filled the streets, echoing and bouncing off the walls. Viola had grown used to the frequent crash-bang-wallop of London life, but Walpole the cat, however, was scared witless and jumped to his feet, darting into the crowd before Viola could say goodbye to the little creature who had captured her heart.

# Chapter Four
*The Lady and the Tarot*

One of the jobs that Viola detested the most was sweeping the bakery floor. It was an endless task. As soon as the floor was clean and shiny, another few customers would come in and leave muddy footprints, or drag in a hundred wet leaves. Of course, her father's baking was forever puffing white flour up into the air, so the floor was constantly coated in a layer of pale dust. Viola had given up telling Teddy that it was fruitless – her brother believed that the shop should look its best at all times. Their father agreed, so unfortunately for her, Viola was stuck sweeping.

*Jangle, jangle, jangle...*

Viola's head darted towards the bakery door as she saw a flash of emerald green disappear down Cobble Lane. Viola looked back to check her father and brother were distracted - which they were thanks to the latest batch of bread, and she quietly placed the broom against the wall. She rushed out of the shop and across the busy street, keeping her eyes fixed on the alleyway.

After following the jingle jangle of the bells on the woman's shawl down the long, narrow alley, Viola stopped suddenly. She had caught up with the Emerald Lady far quicker than she had imagined and so she dashed into a divot in the wall to use as a hiding place. She slowly peered around the wall to see the Emerald Lady speaking with a short, grubby man that Viola hadn't seen before.

"You got the ale?" the lady asked, holding her hand out. The impossibly thin man was dressed in a scruffy, grey suit with shabby, fingerless gloves. His trousers were caked with mud at the ankles and he looked dreadfully tired. He coughed heavily before answering.

"Aye, I said I'd get it, did I not?" he barked, handing over a large bottle of brown liquid. The woman popped the cork out of the neck and sniffed. She smiled before replacing the stopper and putting the bottle in her huge bag.

"Then I shall begin." She waved him over to three upturned wooden boxes a few feet away from them in the shadowy alleyway. The Emerald Lady sat on one of the crates, sweeping her shawl around her shoulders whilst the grubby man sat on another with the third box nestled between them. She pulled out of her bag a pack of cards – cards which Viola had never seen before – and spread them on the makeshift table. They weren't the sort of playing cards that her father used when he went to the White Bear pub to play a few games with the men of London; these were bigger and had strange multi-coloured pictures on them.

"Pick three of 'em," the woman sniffed. The man took his time, rubbing his hands together as he considered which ones to choose. Eventually, he stabbed three of them with his short, sticklike fingers. The woman turned the first card over, humming slightly as she did so. "The Emperor card...interestin'. I see an old man, an old man with a grey beard. A father, perhaps," the woman said in a thick, deep voice.

"Yes! Why, me pa had a grey beard," the man said, followed by another hacking cough. The Emerald Lady nodded slowly. She tutted before speaking.

"He knows what you're up to, Fred. He knows you're up to no good and he ain't happy," she sighed, looking at the man.

"Liar!" he boomed, throwing his fist onto the crate causing the cards to jump slightly in the air. Viola bit her lip, sensing the immediate tension.

"Wash your mouth out, Frederick White! I ain't no liar. I speak to the dearly departed, I swear. If you don't believe me-" she said sharply.

Viola frowned. Did she mean dead people?

*That's impossible. You can't speak to the dead.*

"Nah, I weren't talking about you, lovey. I meant 'im. I meant me father," he panicked, raising his hands defensively. "He was just as wicked as I am. In fact, he was worse. He was a nasty old man who was nothin' but trouble. I'm an honest fella. Really, I am. Most of the time, anyways."

"I don't need the cards to tell me who you are or what you're up to. You're back to grave robbin', ain't ya?" she asked firmly. Fred looked to the ground.

Viola gasped, throwing her hand over her mouth.

*Grave robbing?* That was a truly horrible crime.

"Don't judge me. I ain't got no money. I need all I can get," he said, sounding desperate. The woman turned over the next card with a smile.

"The Fool," she said, pointing to the card which had a very childlike picture of a jester drawn on it. "Spontaneity and energy. That means you think quickly and get yourself out of all sorts of scrapes."

"True. I get that from me father too. He could talk himself out of anythin'. Anythin' except death, of course."

The third and final card, The Moon, revealed that Fred had something troubling on his mind. According to the Emerald Lady, it had been keeping him awake at night. Fred nodded and explained that his father had died a few months ago from cholera, an utterly horrible illness. Since then, Fred had been looking after his sickly mother but he didn't have enough money to eat, let alone feed his poorly mother, or his wife and two young children. So, in a bid to try and make some much-needed money, he had started going to cemeteries at night and digging up the coffins to look for any jewellery or gold teeth that he could pinch and sell on. Viola closed her eyes as he described the horrors he had done.

*That's why his ankles were so muddy.*

"Your father is tellin' me that you need to look in the red box under his bed. He says you will find somethin' very interestin' in there," the Emerald Lady said, scooping up all the cards. Fred leaned in towards her.

"Really?" he asked, shocked.

"Have a look under his bed and tell me if your old man was being truthful," she smiled, putting the cards on the table.

Suddenly, from the shadows of the long, dark alley came the booming voice of Constable Clancy.

"Gypsy! I know what you're up to! If I catch you, you'll be in trouble yet again!"

The Emerald Lady and Fred both jumped to their feet. In the commotion, Fred knocked over the boxes, causing the cards to fall all over the floor.

"Back slang it!" the Lady cried to Fred, pointing to the other end of the alley. Fred, nodded and ran into the darkness. The Lady swung the bag round onto her shoulder, scooped up the cards and raced after him.

Viola glanced over at the crates left behind and noticed that the Lady had missed three of her cards – they were trapped underneath one of the boxes. Nervous that Constable Clancy was getting ever closer, and suddenly feeling a strange sense of loyalty to the Lady, she ran to the cards and pulled them free from under the crates.

"Miss Pumpernickel?" Constable Clancy asked, seeing her for the first time.

"Hello, sir!" Viola chirped, spinning round to face him.

"What are you doing here?" he asked, trying to peer round her back. "And what have you got in your hands?"

"I don't know what you are talking about, sir. Good day!" she shrugged. He raised an eyebrow and clicked his fingers.

"Viola…"

She knew he was serious so she reluctantly obliged.

"I found them on the floor. Honest," she said, showing him the contents of her hand. He took them from her and studied each one.

"Viola, this woman is very dangerous. And these cards are the work of the devil. You mustn't play with them."

"I wasn't. I found them here and picked them up. I wasn't going to do anything with them, I promise," Viola said honestly. She had no intention of trying to use them, they looked rather scary in her opinion.

"You shouldn't be playing in the backstreets like this. Not on your own. Run along home and we'll say no more about it," he said softly.

"What about the cards?" she asked.

"I'll deal with them. You mustn't mix with such characters as that gypsy woman. Do you understand me?" he asked firmly. Viola nodded and turned away. As she walked out of the alley, she smiled to herself, holding a lone card that she'd smuggled away in her pocket.

# Chapter Five
## *Walpole, the Hero*

Making her way back to the bakery, hoping that her family hadn't noticed that she was missing, Viola spotted Walpole the cat perched on the doorstep of their shop. The bell on his collar sparkled in the sunlight as he sat grooming his paws. Viola smiled and crouched down to the cat, stroking his warm, soft fur.

"Oi, leave off!" Albert cried, gently pushing the cat with his broom. "That pesky thing has been hounding me for hours. Don't you go encouraging him, Viola," he said, shaking his head.

"But Walpole's my friend," Viola said, watching as the little chap scampered off to hide behind a market stall and continue his grooming routine, probably used to being moved along by angry shopkeepers.

"Walpole? Strange name for a cat!" Mr Pumpernickel said, raising an eyebrow. "Just keep him out of the shop. I don't think our customers would fancy a mouthful of cat fur in their scones, do you?

Here, you can carry on with this," he said, handing her the broom. Viola sighed and slumped against the wall. Noticing that his daughter seemed less than excited about the idea of sweeping the floor again, Mr Pumpernickel crouched down to be level with her.

"Once you've finished, how about I take you to the sweetshop?" he whispered. Viola looked up at her father and smiled as he lightly tapped her on the head. After the day she'd had, a bag of pear drops would be very welcome indeed.

Mr Pumpernickel stood, letting out a quiet moan as he did so, and returned to his work. His back was aching after such a long day on his feet and, as much as he would never admit it, he wasn't as young as he wished. As he walked back into the shop, a large, burly man arrived and followed him in. He was dressed from top to toe in dark grey clothes and had a rather dreadful looking scar that ran from his eyebrow to his chin. Viola could just about hear their conversation and it didn't seem to make much sense. Mr Pumpernickel seemed rather angry and kept telling this man that he wasn't interested in his help and to leave him alone. The stranger, however, spoke quietly but firmly. Viola shuffled a little closer to the door and pushed her ear to the small gap.

"You'll regret this, Pumpernickel," the Scarred Man in Grey hissed.

"Get out. I won't tell you again. I will not tolerate being spoken to like this, and in my own shop, nonetheless. Get. Out," he growled through gritted teeth. The Scarred Man in Grey sighed and muttered something rather rude under his breath before storming towards the door. Viola quickly shuffled back and pretended to be incredibly interested in a stone on the floor as the man bundled passed her. She turned and peered through the doorway at her father. Mr Pumpernickel held a large rolling pin above his head for just a second, before letting it fall to the counter. He sighed and wiped his brow on his sleeve. Viola frowned.

*Strange*, she thought as Walpole jogged back to her and nuzzled up against her feet, purring as he pushed his cheek against her ankle boots.

"I'll try and sneak you some food later, little one," she whispered, stroking his head. He looked up at her and let out a soft cry of thanks. Viola smiled and put her finger to her lips.

"Ssssh!" she giggled. "It's our little secret." She stood up and went into the shop, broom in hand, as Walpole waited patiently for any food scraps to come his way.


Having eaten a dinner consisting of offal and potatoes (her least favourite meal but she was so hungry she would have eaten an old sock) and played a few games with her brothers, Viola had finally gone to bed. She wasn't feeling very tired but she was desperate to be alone to look at the Emerald Lady's card. Happy that Teddy had fallen asleep in the rickety old bunk bed above her, Viola quietly climbed out and snuck into the living room, picking up a candle on her way.

Sitting cross-legged on the floor, Viola stared at the peculiar image on the card for the first time, using the candle light to see it through the darkness.

Viola gasped.

It showed a man dressed in a long, black cloak brandishing a large blade staring sinisterly at her. It was truly terrifying. Why did the Emerald Lady have such a scary card in her collection? Maybe Constable Clancy was right – maybe she wasn't the sort of person Viola should be friends with.

*Tap, tap, tap.*

Viola jumped as a rattle on the window broke the silence of the night. They lived above the bakery, so no one could knock on the window, unless they were twenty feet tall, of course.

*Tap, tap, tap.*

Viola stood, holding the candle. She considered calling out to her father or brothers for help, but she didn't want to have to explain why she had the creepy card. She slowly pulled the curtain back to reveal Walpole sitting on the outside ledge, scratching at the glass. Viola looked back towards her parents' room before shoo-ing Walpole to move along. He jumped down to the next level but looked back at Viola with a cry.

"What is it, boy?" she whispered.

Perhaps, Viola thought, he wanted more food. She had managed to sneak him some scraps of offal meat after dinner but maybe it wasn't enough for him. She opened the window to get closer to Walpole.

"What do you want, little 'un?" she asked quietly. He looked down at the street below and then turned back to her.

*He wanted her to follow him.*

It was so dark and cold outside that Viola didn't want to leave the warmth of her home.

"I can't come with you, Walpole. I'm not allowed to go out at night time," she whispered firmly. The cat let out a little cry and made his way down to the street, glancing back at her after every few steps. Her whole body felt a pang of sadness for him. She continued to watch as he cascaded down to the street, worried that he would hurt himself negotiating such difficult jumps. As he finally reached Brookwater Lane's cobbled paving, he disappeared into the smoky darkness. Viola frowned as he seemed to vanish into thin air, wondering why he had wanted her to follow him so badly.

A few seconds of stillness passed before Viola saw it.

A dark figure slowly made his way up the lane, peering into each shop as he passed. Viola watched as he stopped outside Barnaby's Butchers, opposite the bakery, and looked in there for much longer than he did with the others. After a second, having checked he was alone, he thrust his elbow through the glass and reached in, unlocking the door in one slick and seamless move. Within seconds he had opened the door and was in. Viola froze on the spot, unable to take her eyes off the butcher's door.

Without warning, Walpole jumped down from a ledge near the butchers and landed on a mountain of wooden crates with a crash. The sudden noise caused the mysterious man, who was only in the butchers for a moment, to burst into the street in a panic. This time, however, he was holding a huge leg of meat, so huge in fact it was almost bigger than he was.

Viola gasped. As he turned to face the bakery, she could see his face for the first time. It was the man who robbed the watchmakers and set it alight!

Before she knew it, Viola had pulled on her boots, thrown her mother's shawl over her shoulders and dashed to the front door, desperate to get to the street before the villain escaped but knew that she mustn't wake her parents.

Viola quietly closed the front door and instantly regretted it. The cold air hit her tiny frame like a runaway horse. Her freezing throat struggled for air as she desperately sucked in a breath. She yearned for her warm bed and wondered why on earth she ever left it. Realising that she had to move, she ran down the concrete steps to the street, hoping that the thief was still there. She stopped and looked in all directions, squinting her eyes to see through the foggy night air.

The street was dark and silent, save for the whistle of the cold wind. Never had Viola been outside this late at night before and her eyes struggled to adjust to the dark, murky sky. She took a few uneasy steps towards Cobble Lane alley which was still illuminated from the oil lamps hanging on the walls, thanks to the Lamplighter who had been busy lighting them as dusk fell. Viola often watched as the mysterious man would roam the streets, holding a long pole on his shoulder, lighting the lamps of London. He was never seen during the day and always disappeared just as quickly as he arrived. Viola imagined he lived in a tiny cottage and slept all day, waking just before his supper (consisting of a meat pie and a cup of hot tea) before heading out to light the way for the people of London town.

"Walpole?" she called quietly. Shielding her candle from the wind, she moved further again. "Walpole? Where are you, boy?" she whispered.

*Jangle, jangle, jangle...*

Viola's eyes stared at the alley, fear engulfing her body.

A hand grabbed her shoulder and Viola let out a scream, a scream so loud that it echoed through the street and bounced off the walls. She spun around, completely unprepared for whatever horror was about to greet her.

"You shouldn't be 'ere," the Emerald Lady whispered, still gripping her tightly by the shoulder. Terrified, Viola pushed past her and ran hurriedly back to her house, dropping the candle to the ground. She couldn't bring herself to check if she was being followed, she just knew she had to get home as soon as she could. Without the light from her candle, Viola struggled to make out the steps and missed several on her frantic climb, slipping and tripping. Several times she scraped her knees but she didn't care; she had to escape the terrifying Emerald Lady.

Finally, she reached her front door, bursting through it to safety. She slammed the door shut and raced to the living room. Her chest thumped as she desperately pulled off the shawl. Her knees were stinging from the step's blitz attack.

"Viola? What are you doing?" Teddy appeared in the doorway to their bedroom, half asleep. "I heard a noise."

"I – I had a bad dream." Viola decided that perhaps her sibling could do without another one of her tales of adventure. He rubbed his tired eyes as he walked further into the room.

"Why do you have your boots on?"

Viola looked down, realising she had forgotten to take them off in her haste to escape the Lady.

"My feet were cold," she lied, walking past Teddy and back into their bedroom. Teddy watched her leave the room, unsure of what his sister had told him. In the silence, he heard the curtain blowing in the cold night wind. As he reached out for the handle to close the window, he saw her.

The Emerald Lady stood in the street below looking up at Teddy. She nodded at him, wrapped her shawl tightly across her body and disappeared down Cobble Lane. Teddy closed the window, pulled the curtain across and frowned. He'd have to keep an eye on this peculiar woman and make sure no harm came to his little sister.

# Chapter Six
*Digby and the Docklands*

Viola was in a bit of a daze the following morning. Not only because she didn't get much sleep but because she was petrified of seeing the Emerald Lady again. Viola was convinced that she knew she had taken her card and she didn't want her parents thinking she was a whizzer. That would be just dreadful.

Word had quickly spread about the break-in at Barnaby's Butchers. According to Mr Barnaby, the police believed that whoever was behind the crime was also responsible for the robberies and subsequent fires at the bookshop and watchmakers. They reckoned that the robber had been disturbed and ran away before he could do much damage to the butchers. Viola smiled to herself as she thought of Walpole jumping into the crates and wondered if, somehow, he knew what he was doing in bringing the robbery to a swift end.

She sat on the step of the bakery, carefully watching for any sign of the Emerald Lady so she could make a quick getaway. She kept the card in her apron pocket for safe keeping. It wasn't the sort of thing you could just leave lying around, you know.

Brookwater Lane seemed rather quiet. Not a lot of people were visiting the market which meant that, in turn, not a lot of people would visit the bakery. One person that Viola did see, however, was the perfectly horrid Digby Travers.

Digby was the same age as Teddy and in fact, used to be close friends with him. They were both considered good natured boys until Digby began to cause trouble. He would bully smaller children and tried to encourage Teddy to do the same. Teddy, being a kind soul, refused to join in the horrible bullying and stood up to him. Digby called Teddy a coward and the two of them were no longer friends. Teddy would often tell Viola that Digby hated the world and everyone in it. As such, he had been known to associate with petty criminals and, on many occasions, had been accused of stealing. Somehow, he always got away with his crimes, however, and the police were never able to prove that he was ever guilty of any wrong doing.

Digby worked as a street sweeper and operated down Brookwater Lane, amongst others. He was lazy and mean and would often glare at Viola as he swept past the shop. Once he even swept a huge cloud of dirt onto Viola as she sat on the step. He found it utterly hilarious when poor Viola coughed and spluttered, and simply carried on his business rather than trying to help her. As I say, a perfectly horrid boy.

Viola wasn't in the mood to deal with Digby today and he seemed to feel the same. He looked over at her but instead of saying anything mean, he stuck his tongue out and passed her without any trouble. She responded by glaring at him as he walked by and whispering under her breath.

"*Beastly boy.*"

As Digby passed Pumpernickel's Bakery, out of the corner of her eye, Viola spotted Walpole drinking some milk from a saucer that one of the other shopkeepers had kindly put out for him. Viola stood and made her way over. He sensed her next to him and stopped drinking to look up at her. The milk was splashed into his ginger fur which made him look like he had a tiny silver beard. Walpole meowed and turned to walk away.

"I'm coming with you this time, little one," Viola said loudly. She didn't care who heard her talking to a cat, she needed to follow him. He picked up the pace to a trot and Viola started to jog behind him. She didn't realise how fast cats could move when they wanted.

She followed him past many shops and eventually out of Brookwater Lane. They went over the stone bridge that Mr Pumpernickel had always told her was "exceptionally dangerous" and through the long, bustling street that finally lead to the docklands.

The harbour was busy and loud with ship bells ringing out every few seconds. There were lots of angry looking men shouting instructions at each other to do this and do that, pull this and pull that, getting various ships and boats ready to set sail. Walpole, however, seemed completely unfazed by the frantic scene ahead of them as he continued to maze his way through the hordes of people. Viola tried to keep up with him but being so slight, she was almost pushed over by the oncoming crowd, most of whom were far too busy to notice her.

Suddenly, Walpole jumped into the air, obviously spooked by something, and launched himself high onto a wall. Desperate to follow him, Viola ran to keep up, checking now and again to make sure he was still in sight. As she fought to stay with him, her feet became entangled in some large, heavy cargo rope that was gathered on the floor. Her feet locked in the rope but unfortunately her body kept moving. With nowhere else to go, she fell to the floor with a thud, yelping out in pain.

Walpole, sensing something was wrong with his new friend, jumped down and mewed as he approached her.

"I'm alright," Viola sighed, managing to pull her ankle free from the rope. "Go on, boy. I'll follow you - but not so fast this time." As she stood, her ankle throbbed under her weight but she was determined to carry on and find out whatever it was that Walpole was so desperate to show her.

Eventually she made it through the swarm of people and found Walpole sitting on a large boulder, staring at her. Viola leaned against it to catch her breath. She reached out and gently rubbed his head, his loud purrs indicating that he was enjoying the comfort of her touch.

Viola stood and watched the huge ships and small wooden boats bobbing about on the choppy water. The strong smell of salt water filled her nostrils. It was a pleasant change from the dreadful, stifling odour of the London streets.

"Now that I've followed you here, what do you want with me?" Viola asked, after a moment.

"It's me who wants ya," came a voice from behind her. Viola turned quickly to see the Emerald Lady standing right behind her. She instinctively put her hand to her pocket, worried that the Emerald Lady knew that her card was in there.

"Oh...h-hello," Viola eventually managed to stutter, her voice almost trapped in her throat. The Lady gave a nasally laugh that made Viola feel rather nauseous. It reminded her of one of her father's customers, Mr Glenn, who used to eat tobacco and spit it out into the street. Her mother would often tut when he left the shop and had warned her children to steer clear of that particular fellow.

"I see you've met my Walpole," the Emerald Lady said, putting her huge handbag on the ground. Within seconds, Walpole had jumped down and curled up inside it. Viola's heart sank.

*How could such a gorgeous little creature belong to such a terrifying woman?*

"I didn't know he was your cat. I'm sorry," she said, her voice trembling.

"I believe you have something of mine." The Lady held out a gloved hand. Viola took a breath and slowly pulled out the card. She looked at Walpole who, by now, was grooming himself, no doubt in readiness for a nap. Seeing him calm and content somehow reassured Viola that she was safe. For now, at least.

"I didn't steal it," Viola whimpered. "I found it in the alleyway and had picked it up to give it back to you, I promise, but then Constable Clancy found me and I-" she babbled, handing the card over to her.

"I know, Viola. I know," she interrupted. Viola frowned.

"How do you know my name?"

"I know all about you, Miss Pumpernickel," the Lady said craftily. "You see, I know all about everyone."

"Really?" Viola asked, confused and amazed by such a statement.

"I've been around London longer than I care to remember. I know everyone's business – even after they've passed over to the heavens. It's rather bothersome at times, I can tell ya. Never get a moment's peace."

She explained to Viola that she had a handful of rather peculiar talents. One of these talents was that she could read people's minds. Not all the time, you must understand, but every now and again if her brain wasn't too tired and the other person had an honest, open mind. On the odd occasion, she was even able to read the minds of people less honest and open, but that was far harder and required a lot of concentration on her part, and concentration was not something she had a lot of, I can tell you.

She was also a psychic fortune teller, which meant that she could speak to people who had died, or "passed over" as she called it. Ever since she was little, she explained that she could communicate with the dead, whether she wanted to or not. No one else seemed able to hear these voices, but time after time, the Emerald Lady proved to those who didn't believe her that she knew things that only the spirits knew.

"Is that why you spoke to that man in the alley?" Viola was shocked. Her voice had gone a little higher than before.

"I knew you was watchin'," the Lady smiled. "You shouldn't sneak around like that. It ain't safe in these streets." She put the card back in her bag.

"I know, I know," Viola sighed. "Whizzers and maltoolers, whatever they are."

"Criminal folk, Viola. Pickpockets, cheats. The bad people of London," the Lady sniffed. Walpole, meanwhile, was fast asleep. Viola smiled.

"He must have been tired," Viola said, pointing to the cosy looking cat. The Lady nodded.

"He works very hard, does Walpole. He's my little guardian angel," the Lady replied. Viola was convinced she saw a tear glisten in her eye. A moment's silence passed between them, as they sat watching the ships bob up and down.

"You 'ungry?" the Lady asked, plunging her hand into her dress pocket. Viola nodded, she hadn't eaten since the early morning and her tummy was starting to growl. The Emerald Lady pulled out one of the biggest oranges Viola had ever seen and handed it to the little girl. Viola looked down at the huge fruit that she needed both hands to hold and gulped. She tried to pierce the skin but it was far too tough for her slight fingers. The Emerald Lady smiled and took the fruit back. She pulled off her gloves and jabbed her thumb into the centre of the orange, pulling its skin away. Viola glanced over at the still snoozing cat and smiled, remembering what her father had said.

*Strange name for a cat.*

The Emerald Lady gasped.

"You wash your mouth out! Robert Walpole was Britain's first Prime Minister, I'll have you know. He should be remembered – he should be respected," she said. Viola looked up at her shocked.

"How did you know what I was thinking?"

"I told you, I know things," the Emerald Lady smiled, handing Viola a chunk of orange. She put it straight into her mouth and smiled as the juice burst through the orange and down her chin. Viola giggled as she wiped her mouth with the back of her hand.

After a while, knowing now that the Emerald Lady perhaps wasn't as scary as she first thought, Viola realised that she didn't know her real name. Before she had time to ask, the Emerald Lady had responded.

"Bertha. Bertha Bard," she smiled, holding out her hand which was covered in brightly coloured rings. Her wrist carried lots of silver bracelets and bangles that sparkled in the sun.

"Viola Pumpernickel – but you already knew that," Viola giggled, shaking her hand. "Can I ask, why did Walpole bring me here?"

"There is a thief roamin' our streets, Viola. A thief who is worse than most of the others combined. He's stealin' whatever he pleases from whoever he pleases and when he's done, he burns the place to the ground. Evil personified. He robbed the bookshop, the watchmakers and you saw him last night at the butchers, didn't ya?"

"And the watch shop," Viola whispered. The Lady nodded.

"This villain steals what he likes and then sells whatever he's got here at the docks. There are so many people here that no one knows who is who and what is what, and no one cares to ask. Your father's barrow would have made a very good carriage for what he was looting. He may be a thief but he's resourceful!"

"You should tell Constable Clancy about this. He'll know how to catch him," Viola exclaimed. Bertha put her hand up and shook her head.

"Oh, he already knows this is where the criminal folk come to do business. Anyway, in my experience, the police don't believe people like us."

"People like *us*?" Viola repeated, confused.

"Some people don't like it when girls ask questions. They think we should just sit still and stay quiet. But I've never been quiet in me whole life and I don't think you have, either."

"No, I haven't. My mother says I have a busy imagination and Father Kelly calls me a chatterbox," she smiled. Bertha touched her hand.

"You remind me of my girl, Isobel."

"Do I?" Viola chirped. "Maybe we can play together one day."

Bertha fell silent.

"Isobel is with the angels, my love," she said solemnly. Viola knew what that meant. Her grandfather was with the angels too.

"Oh, I'm terribly sorry."

"Nay bother." Bertha shook her head as if trying to shake the memory away. "I got you here today because I need your 'elp."

"Me? How can I help?"

"You, Viola Pumpernickel, are going to help me catch the thief of Brookwater Lane," Bertha said, putting an orange segment in her mouth and rubbing her bejewelled hands together.

Ten minutes later, Viola stood next to Bertha, watching the dock workers load up their cargo on the various boats. Bertha had told her that the infamous thief would be there soon and to keep her eyes peeled.

So, Viola did just that.

She looked at every person that walked by but so far there hadn't been any sign of him. Every thirty seconds, Viola would tell Bertha that he wasn't there yet, despite her watching for him too.

"So, Viola. What do you want to do when you're grown?" Bertha asked.

"I used to want to be a dancer or a singer. But now I want to be the police, like Constable Clancy. I want to make London a better place," she said looking up at the Lady who nodded in response.

"And that can only be a good thing. There are too many liars and thieves in these parts."

"*You're* a liar and a thief," Viola replied bluntly causing Bertha to choke on her orange. "I've heard people say that fortune tellers prey on people who are grieving and swindle them out of money. Constable Clancy told me you're a charlatan and that I am not to talk to you."

"And is that what you believe, little 'un?" she asked, just about recovered from her choking episode. Viola shrugged but before she had a chance to speak, she grabbed Bertha's arm and pointed down to the whizzer who was walking along the docks pushing a wheelbarrow – her father's no doubt - full of hessian sacks.

"There he is!" Viola gasped. He wore the same muddy boots and scruffy, torn naval jacket that he had worn during the robbery of the watchmakers. He stopped by a wooden crate and started to empty the contents of the sacks on to it. He turned and called out to a few men who soon surrounded him, keen to see what he was selling. Once his audience were assembled, he opened the sacks and pulled

out several slabs of meat wrapped in scraps of fabric.

"He stole that from the butchers last night! He must have chopped it up," Viola cried, before being shushed by Bertha.

"He's selling the meat on to those men. He'll make a handsome amount of money today," Bertha whispered. Viola watched the man hand out the meat in exchange for handfuls of money. The men all seemed happy with their purchases and one by one, they left the man. Once his sacks were empty, the man threw them into the wheelbarrow. A smile had spread across his face and he was obviously satisfied with his day's work. He turned and made his way back through the ever-growing crowd.

"He's leaving!" Viola cried, looking up at Bertha. She nodded.

"Walpole will follow him," Bertha said, watching as the cat suddenly woke, jumped out of the bag and darted after the thief. "Be safe, my boy."

Viola watched as the daring cat zig-zagged his way through

people, dogs, carts and various other hazards to catch up with the thief.

"We can't let him get away."

"He won't. Walpole will tell us, when the time is right, where this thief is and we will take action. But for now, you should return home. We've done all we can for today," Bertha said gently.

Constable Clancy was waiting with Mr and Mrs Pumpernickel in the bakery when Viola finally returned. As soon as she saw Viola appear, her mother rushed to her.

"Where have you been?" Mrs Pumpernickel cried, grabbing her daughter and pulling her in for the biggest hug Viola had ever had. Her eyes looked tired and watery.

"I went for a stroll. Why are you crying?" Viola asked, pulling herself out of the hug to face her mother. Tears were streaming down her pale face. "Is Rupert poorly again?"

"No, my darling. Rupert is quite well," Mr Pumpernickel said, gently stroking Viola's blonde hair. "It's you we were worried about, my love."

"Me?" Viola was confused. They had no reason to worry about her. Mrs Pumpernickel stood and wiped her cheeks. Constable Clancy coughed and removed his hat.

"Viola, your parents were concerned that you had not been home for some time. A few hours, in fact. Where have you been?" he asked gently.

"I went to the docklands," Viola answered. Her mother gasped.

"The docklands? But they are so far away!" her father said, sounding more than a little worried. "Far away and dangerous! You should not go there alone, my girl."

"I wasn't alone. I was with the Emerald Lady."

Her mother sighed and turned away from Viola. Her father put a hand on his wife's shoulder and shook his head. Constable Clancy was the first to speak.

"Who is this Emerald Lady, Viola?"

"She is the fortune teller, the gypsy."

Clancy raised his hand to calm Mary and gently asked Viola to tell them exactly what had happened.

So, she did.

She told them about the Emerald Lady and her strange cards, Walpole the cat, the burglar and the docklands. She explained that Bertha could speak to the dead and would help those who lost a family member or dear friend find peace. Not everyone believed Bertha, of course. Some people were dreadfully mean and would even throw things at her in the street or shout rude words at her. She had become tough over the years and no longer stood for any sort of bullying. She had to give the impression she was mean and horrid to protect herself. Viola felt very sorry for the poor woman. She couldn't imagine being bullied so badly that she had to pretend to be unpleasant and scary to stop it.

Mrs Pumpernickel didn't look at Viola as she spoke.

"- and Bertha, or the Emerald Lady, well, she asked me to help her catch the thief and I think I'm going to," Viola said, coming to the end of her report.

"The docklands are no place for a young girl, Viola. Neither's policing. If I were you, I would steer clear of the Emerald Lady, as you call her, and her dangerous plans. I know all about her, Viola, and she's a liar. People like her deal in fakery and satanic agencies. She is not to be trusted," Clancy said firmly.

"Satanic? She's nothing of the sort!" Viola protested.

"Listen to the policeman, Viola. Please," Mary snapped. Viola pursed her lips, shocked at her mother's outburst.

"The streets of London are bursting at the seams with thieves and it is *my* job to catch them, not *yours*. You stay here with your father and help the family business. Leave the unfavourables to me," the policeman said firmly. He didn't have the same friendly tone as he usually had when speaking to Viola, and she didn't like it very much. However, she knew she couldn't win this argument, so she reluctantly nodded. Constable Clancy nodded back and put his hat on. After a moment, Viola spoke again.

"I saw him wearing the same coat he wore when he robbed the watchmakers. The coat that lost the button I gave you. It's the same man, I promise."

"Leave him to me. I mean it, Viola. You have no idea who you are dealing with. You're just a girl," Clancy sighed, turning to her parents. He muttered a goodbye and Mr Pumpernickel thanked him for his help. As the policeman left the shop, Mrs Pumpernickel turned away from Viola and disappeared out to the back of the bakery. Viola sighed. Although she was upset that her mother was feeling so sad, she knew that she would understand the truth soon enough.   One thing was now certain in Viola's mind, if she and Bertha were going to catch the thief, they'd have to do it without the help of the police for a little while.

# Chapter Seven
## *The Cabin in the Woods*

It was dark and rainy and the night air was colder than Viola could remember it ever being. Her mother had made a delicious tomato soup for the family dinner along with leftover bread from the bakery and it really was scrummy.

As the children went to bed one by one that evening, their father had given them an extra blanket each to keep warm and their mother had made a hot spicy drink, using some fruits she had bought from the market that day. Viola didn't much like the taste and it burnt her tongue a little, but she was glad of the much-needed warmth it provided.

Although a good few days had passed since she had met with Bertha at the docklands, Viola lay in her bed thinking about the Emerald Lady and the 'whizzer' as Bertha continued to call him. She used some very peculiar words sometimes. Viola didn't understand all of them but they certainly made her chuckle. She had been thinking about how they could catch this villain in the act and show Constable Clancy just what this thief was up to.

As she lay in the darkness, she could hear her father's deep snores resonating from the other bedroom. She often heard his snores and wondered how her mother and Rupert could possibly sleep through it. Sharing a room with Teddy, she was thankful he hadn't inherited their father's habit in that regard.

A strange noise from outside made her jump. For a moment, she thought that somebody had knocked on the shop door but she knew it was far too late for anyone to fancy some sultana and banana bread. She peered up at her brother who seemed undisturbed. She quietly peeled the blanket off and crept over to the window. She pulled back the curtain, expecting to see Walpole on the sill again. However, this time it was something far more worrying.

The whizzer stood in the street below, shifting from one leg to the other in a bid to stay warm. Viola held her breath, afraid that he could hear her. He stood next to a large brown sack, full to the brim. The fog over London was so thick that Viola struggled to make out what was happening. A few seconds passed before he was joined by another man, a man much taller and slender than him. He opened the bag and peered inside. The pair spoke for a moment or two before the thin man suddenly pushed the whizzer. It was with such force that he staggered backwards, almost onto his back. Viola gasped and, fearing she would wake her brother, covered her mouth with her hand. The pair of men started brawling in the street – punches, kicks, slaps; the fight was brutal. The thin man pushed the whizzer once again and, this time the whizzer fell to the ground.

The thin man laughed at his opponent and held out a hand. The whizzer sighed and reached into his pocket for a large wad of cash. The thin man grabbed it and stuffed it into his jacket pocket. He said something obviously very nasty to the whizzer, who was still lying on the ground, picked up the sack, and left. The whizzer slowly stood and, clutching his side, scurried off into the darkness like a wounded animal.

Viola watched in silence, concerned about what she had just seen, as Bertha emerged through the fog. Viola's jaw dropped.

*What was she doing?*

It wasn't safe for her to be there alone. If the men came back and realised she had been watching them, they could very well attack her too. Viola knew she had to help Bertha. She spun on her heel and quietly made her way to the door. She thrust her feet into her black boots, grabbed her woollen shawl and red coat – she didn't want to forget that again - and disappeared out of the bedroom. She peered back at her brother to make sure she hadn't woken him.

Teddy was in a deep sleep and their father's snores continued to ring out from his room, so Viola crept out of the front door. She knew she shouldn't be doing it again and if her parents caught her she would be in deep trouble, but she knew she had to find out more about this thief. She had to prove to her parents and Constable Clancy that she and Bertha were telling the truth.

The freezing cold air took Viola's breath away, her bones shuddered as she gathered enough courage to move. She ran down the steps and over to where Bertha had been standing. However, the street was now empty. She turned and tried to see through the fog.

"Go back to bed, Viola," the Emerald Lady hissed from behind her, clutching an oil lamp.

"I saw him, Bertha. I saw the whizzer again. He had a fight with another man and he's–"

"Go home," Bertha repeated. "I saw the whole thing. In fact, I've sent Walpole off to follow him. He will report back to me soon. Get yourself home, girl."

"I want to come with you. I cannot let you go on your own. Not now we know he is so vicious." Viola's teeth chattered.

After a moment, Bertha sighed.

"Here," she said peeling off her fingerless gloves and handing them to her. "You'll need these."

They had been walking for ages. Viola was cold and tired but she daren't tell the Emerald Lady that she wanted to go home. Not after she kicked up such a fuss to come along with her in the first place. They were following Walpole who, in turn, had been following the whizzer from Brookwater Lane. Viola wondered just how much further they had to go but trusted that Walpole knew what he was doing.

After a while, they found themselves walking through Hyde Park which meant that they were near Kensington Palace, a grand and magnificent house where Queen Victoria used to live. Viola's father would often walk her and the boys past the magnificent building and they would imagine all the wonderful food and music and dancing and all-round fun going on inside. Viola would often dream about what life would be like if the Pumpernickels lived in Kensington Palace. They would never want for anything with endless laughter and happiness filling the halls. It would be a perfect life, she just knew it.

"Are we nearly there?" Viola whispered as they made their way through the huge park. The Emerald Lady shrugged.

"I cannot say. Walpole will tell us when we're close."

Viola sighed, her feet were starting to ache. Her father would usually carry her on her shoulders at this point in their journey. Somehow, she didn't think she could ask Bertha to do the same.

"It ain't all grand, you know. Living in luxury," Bertha said, out of the blue. Viola frowned.

"What do you mean?"

"You think that money will bring you happiness. True, it will take away a lot of worry from your life but it ain't a magic wand, Viola. Sad things happen to rich people too," she said quietly.

Just then, Walpole stopped in his tracks. His fur stood on end as he turned back to the pair.

"We're here," the Emerald Lady said, instinctively taking Viola's hand. She gulped; what on earth were they going to find?

The sound of a snapping twig made Viola's head turn. Someone was following them, she was sure of it. However, the park looked dark and vacant. The Emerald Lady gently pulled Viola towards Walpole as he looked into the distance, letting out a gentle meow.

"That's where he must live." Bertha pointed at a small and

grotty wooden cabin, almost entirely hidden by thorny bushes and greenery. If it weren't for a candle light flickering in the window, visible through a tiny break in the shrubbery, you wouldn't even know it was there.

"W-what are we g-going to do?" Viola stuttered. She wasn't sure if her shivers were due to her nervousness or the sheer cold. Bertha put a finger to her mouth and shushed

"We must make sure that this is where all his loot is. You know, where he keeps everythin' he pinches. Then we will decide how best to deal with the little swine," Bertha whispered. She put out the light from her lamp, plunging them into near darkness, the full moon providing the only light.

They moved closer to the cabin and, standing on a large grey rock, Viola carefully peered through the grubby cobweb-ridden window. What she saw inside reminded her of the bric-a-brac stall on the market: jewellery, coins, watches and a big fur coat, all shoved carelessly into her father's wheelbarrow covered over by a grotty potato sack. Viola's blood boiled.

"This is definitely the place. This is where he lives!" she wailed. Bertha gasped, grabbing Viola and pulling her away from the window.

"Shush!" she whispered firmly. "Keep your voice down or he'll 'ear ya!"

Her warning was too late however, as the door to the cabin flew open.

"Oi!" the whizzer cried, waving what looked like a walking stick at them. "What's your game?"

"Nothin', nothin'. We apologise, sir. We were lost," Bertha lied. The man obviously didn't believe her.

"You were snoopin' around. Do you know what happens to nosey little snoopers?" he hissed, peering down at Viola who was by now utterly terrified, every bone of her body trembling. Calculating that Viola would probably be his weaker opponent, he grabbed her wrist and pulled her close to him, twisting her arm. She let out a yelp of pain and desperately tried to wriggle free from his grip. Bertha screamed at him to leave her alone, whacking him with her huge bag. He winced and dropped the stick, but didn't lose his hold on Viola. Instead, he pushed Bertha who fell backwards onto the wet grass.

"Nosey little beggars need to learn their place," he hissed.

"Let her go!" came a booming voice from behind them. Teddy emerged from within the dark woodland, his face angrier than Viola had ever seen before. The man laughed.

"Why should I?" he gripped Viola even tighter, making her cry out. Teddy growled, rushing past Bertha and grabbing the man by the collar. The whizzer had no choice but to release Viola, who hurried to the safety of Bertha's side. Teddy pushed the man up against the wall of the cabin. He was obviously shocked and scared by this sudden and violent outburst.

"Leave off! I ain't done nothin' wrong," he whimpered. He had turned from a scary thug into a coward in the blink of an eye.

"Liar!" Viola cried. "You stole from the butchers and you stole from the watchmakers and then you set it on fire! I saw you with my own eyes." She couldn't abide lying and felt she had to make sure her brother knew the truth. "And you probably burnt poor Mr Jeffers' shop to the ground too!"

"You can't prove a thing," the man snarled. Viola raised an eyebrow.

"We found a gold button at the watchmakers. A very distinctive gold button, that I believe matches the buttons on the coat you are wearing this very evening. Teddy? An anchor and crown, I think you'll find."

Teddy looked at his little sister, just for a moment, both surprised and impressed with what she was saying. Still holding the man against the cabin wall, Teddy looked down at the jacket. Sure enough, the buttons were identical - and one was missing from his sleeve. Teddy glared at him.

"This ain't my coat," the man gulped. "I nicked it from a sailor."

"He's lying," Viola said firmly.

"Now, what happens next is up to you," Teddy said to the man, still pinning him against the wall, his feet dangling like a child sitting on a wall. "We either tell our good friend, Constable Clancy about what we've seen here tonight, or you give everything back to their rightful owners tomorrow morning, as soon as we see the sun. Which would you prefer?"

The man laughed.

"What's so funny?" Teddy hissed.

"You have no idea who you're messin' with. You're playing a dangerous game, lad, and there ain't a chance in hell that you'll win."

Frustrated, Teddy gripped the man's collar even tighter and

lifted him higher off the ground. Even though the whizzer was probably twenty years older than Teddy, the youngster was taller and far stronger.

"You're hurting me! Let me go," he cried out.

"Agree to give back everything you have stolen," Teddy snarled.

"Very well. I will give everything back tomorrow. You have my word. Please don't hurt me. I didn't mean nothin' by it."

Teddy sighed and let go of the man who fell to the ground with a thud. He straightened his collar and took a breath to calm down.

"What do you say to my sister?" Teddy hissed.

"Sorry, little lady. I didn't mean to scare ya'."

"What's your name?" Teddy hissed.

"I ain't tellin'," he smirked. Viola rolled her eyes, frustrated at his unhelpful attitude. Bertha raised an eyebrow.

"Wait," she said staring at him rather intently. The man glared at her, unsure of what she was up to. Bertha moved closer to the scoundrel, never taking her eyes off him. He shifted uncomfortably, frowning at her actions. After a few seconds, she smiled. "His name is George Plumb."

"How did you know that?" Plumb gulped.

"She knows *everything*," Viola replied, confidently.

"Nay, she must have heard about me," Plumb shrugged.

"And he likes to chew on his toenails..." Bertha said pulling a disgusted face. Plumb's cheeks reddened.

"Oi! That's private!"

"Come on, Viola, it's time to go home," Teddy said, reaching for her hand. "Remember what I said, Plumb...return the goods or I'll be back with the full force of the law."

He took Viola's hand from Bertha and scooped her up into his arms. She had never been so thankful to see her big brother in all her life. Bertha smiled her gratitude at Teddy as they made their way out of the park, completely unaware that someone was watching them.

Someone far more sinister than a common thief...

# Chapter Eight
*The Governor*

Plumb returned to his cabin and took a huge slug of ale to calm his nerves. Teddy's attack had shaken him to his core. He looked down at the jacket and growled. He pulled it off and threw it to the floor, angry that it had somehow betrayed him.

As he took a second slug of ale, a bang on the door made him jump so high in the air that the beer sloshed out of the bottle and landed on the floor with a splat.

"Y-yes?" he cried, terrified that Teddy had come back.

"Open the door, Plumb, you rotten little weasel," came the snarl of the Governor, his boss. Plumb sighed – he would have preferred Teddy. As he opened the door, the Governor pushed his way into the cabin and signalled for Plumb to close it behind him.

"Would you like a sip of ale?" Plumb asked, showing him the bottle. The Governor scrunched up his nose. It looked like it had been swimming in mud.

"I'm not here to drink with you, Plumb. I'm here for my money," he said, turning to face his little assistant. The Governor was easily six foot tall and so towered above Plumb. He wore very fine, expensive clothes that he cherished. He believed in looking his best and would stop at nothing to do so.

Plumb sighed.

"I ain't got all of it." He reached into his pocket and pulled out a handful of coins. "I couldn't sell all the meat. I 'ad to throw some away as it was rotten."

"You threw it away?" the Governor whispered, horrified. Plumb nodded, afraid to look him in the eye. "Have you learnt nothing from our two years together, Plumb? Have you forgotten who I am?" he hissed. Plumb gulped.

"No, sir. You are the Governor, sir. You look after the people of London - sir."

"Indeed. And therefore, I have a lot of people who owe me some favours. A lot of people who watch dullards like you to make sure you're not trying to fleece me. You wouldn't fleece me now, would you, Plumb?" the Governor asked with a smile. Plumb shook his head. The Governor suddenly grabbed him by the collar. "If you don't give me every last penny from the sale of the meat, I will take you straight down to the police station and make sure you are locked away forever."

Plumb knew that he was a very well-connected man and that this could very easily become a reality.

"I'm sorry. The money - I lost it." Plumb wailed, terrified of the Governor's reaction. "I was robbed just now in Brookwater Lane. It was one of the Black Tile Gang," he said, still being lifted in the air by the Governor. Silence filled the cabin as the Governor's face dropped. The Black Tile Gang were a group of frightening, vicious, highly unreasonable criminals and even the Governor knew he was no match for them. He sighed and let go of Plumb. He paced away from him as he straightened his cravat.

"Who were those people here just now?" he asked, changing the subject.

"Do-gooders," Plumb replied, struggling to stay on his feet. His legs were like jelly after the two attacks. "The girl told me they know what I've been up to. She said she'd seen me stealin'. Then an *enormous* man appeared and said that I have to give everything back or they will tell the old bill - or worse."

"Hmmm," the Governor mused, sitting on the bench. "An enormous man, you say? He looked like a young lad to me. Edward Pumpernickel, in fact. I have socks older than him."

"Was it? It was so dark I could barely see," Plumb lied. His plan for sympathy from the Governor had failed spectacularly.

"Edward and his meddlesome little sister, Viola," the Governor sighed. "And that dreadful, old girl, Bertha Bard. You didn't tell them about me, did you?"

"No, sir! I wouldn't do such a thing. I would never betray you."

The Governor pursed his lips together silently and nodded. He knew he had Plumb wrapped around his little finger.

"The gypsy woman read me mind though," Plumb added. "She knew me name without me sayin' it and she knew I chewed my - " he stopped before he said too much. He didn't think the Governor would approve of his revolting habit. "God only knows what she'd hear if she listened to me thoughts for long enough."

"I doubt she's interested in anything floating around in that head of yours, Plumb. Dull as ditch water," the Governor sneered, looking at his assistant with an expression of sheer dislike. "She probably knows your name because you are famous throughout the whole of London for being the most idiotic creature to ever live."

Plumb sighed and despondently took a swig from his bottle.

"Now, you and I have a problem, Plumb," the Governor continued. "You see, if you can't defend yourself against a couple of silly little children and an old woman, I'm starting to question whether you are the right man for what I have planned."

"I am, sir. I am. Please give me another chance."

The Governor looked him in the eyes for a moment.

"I suppose I could give you...*one* more chance."

Plumb let out a sigh of relief and smiled.

"Thank you, Guv. I mean, *Governor*, I mean, the Governor, *sir*," he spluttered. As the Governor turned to leave the cabin, he peered back at Plumb.

"Make sure that Viola is not one for babbling," the Governor said calmly.

"But Guv, sir, she's just a kid! And as for that gypsy woman, she lies for a livin'! Ain't no one goin' to believe 'em."

"In that case, we must think up some way you can repay the money you owe me. I could chop off your hand - or cut out your tongue?" the Governor grabbed a rusty knife that was in the sink and held it up high. Plumb flinched.

"No, not me tongue!" he cried. "Fine, fine. I'll stop that pesky kid talking but I will 'ave to return a few bits tomorrow, just to be sure. We don't want 'er telling the old bill before I've had a chance to get you your money," he sighed. The Governor smiled and dropped the knife back it the sink with a clang. He straightened his jacket and tie.

"Get Crabtree to help you. He's always very willing. I would oblige but the Pumpernickels know me and I can't risk blowing my cover. I've worked too hard to lose it all because of you."

"Yes, sir."

"Oh, and Plumb? If you set fire to one more shop, you won't live to tell the tale. Understood? I have told you a thousand times, no fires. They're foolish and unpredictable."

"Sorry, sir."

"Those nosey little Pumpernickels will soon wish they never interfered with my business," the Governor laughed, staring out of the window into the night.

"You cannot tell our parents about tonight, Teddy. Promise me?" Viola whispered as they were finally back in their beds. Viola was still shivering from the cold despite having the extra blanket.

"I promise. And you must promise me that you won't go anywhere near that man, Plumb, again," he replied.

"I promise," Viola said firmly. She didn't fancy going back to that dreadful place ever again, thank you very much.

"Or that woman. She is a very bad influence on you, girl."

Viola's heart sank. Bertha was her friend and although she was more than a little scared of her in the beginning, she liked her now and she loved Walpole. The thought of never seeing them again made Viola feel incredibly sad.

As she lay there in silence, replaying the evening's events in her mind, something just didn't feel right. Plumb didn't seem like the sort of man who could orchestrate at least three robberies and avoid capture by the police. He must be working for someone higher up. Someone with a much craftier brain.

"You did make me smile though, Viola. You sounded like a regular constable," Teddy whispered. "You're a very clever girl. Smart as a fox."

Viola giggled as sunlight started to creep through the curtain, meaning their father would be awake soon. She just hoped that Plumb would stick to his word.

Sure enough, the next morning, Albert had gone down to open the bakery for the day to find his wheelbarrow waiting outside the door.

"It's fantastic!" he exclaimed, a smile beaming across his face. He told every single customer that came in that day that the thief had mysteriously returned his barrow and it still worked perfectly.

Viola and Teddy never spoke of the incident again.

# Chapter Nine
## *Florence Bramble*

Today was a very special day. Viola's best friend in the whole world was coming to visit. Florence Bramble, or Flo as everyone called her, had moved away a few months ago when her father tragically died of a very sudden and truly horrible illness. It was a miserable thing and Viola was heartbroken for Flo. When Mr Bramble died, Flo's mother wouldn't eat or sleep or even speak and the doctor said that she needed to go away for a while to get better.

So, Flo's mother went to a special hospital and Flo went to live with her Aunt Eliza in Brighton, down in Sussex. Viola missed Flo terribly so when Mrs Pumpernickel said that Flo was back in London for a while to visit her mother, who was improving greatly, Viola was very excited. She had been sitting on the step of the bakery since sunrise, desperate to see her friend again. She had even asked her mother to wash and prepare her most special dress for the occasion.

"When will she be here, papa?" Viola asked when Albert came to check on his daughter.

"Soon, my darling. She will be here soon," he said gently. He took her hand in his. "Darling, you must understand that Flo may be a little...different since you last saw her."

Viola frowned.

*Different? What on earth did he mean?*

"Her life is no longer how it was. Her father, my dear friend John, passed away and her poor mother has been most unwell. I understand how terrible it is to lose a father when you are so young, so please allow for Flo to be very sad and perhaps not the same girl she was for a while," he said gently. Tears filled Viola's eyes.

"Will she still be my friend?" she asked hopefully. Mr Pumpernickel smiled.

"Of course, my darling." Mr Pumpernickel kissed her on the head. "Just remember that she may not want to play as much as she used to. You will need understanding and patience. Two things I know you have in abundance."

As he uttered those words, the clip clop of a horse and carriage echoed up Brookwater Lane. Mr Pumpernickel smiled and pointed.

"I think she's here," he said. Viola jumped up and raced over to the approaching carriage, Mr Pumpernickel's cries to be careful ringing in her ears. Viola reached the carriage door as it came to a halt. The door opened and a small, gentle looking woman appeared. She wore a large, furry, red coat and her hair was impeccably neat and tidy.

She must be Auntie Eliza.

"Good morning," Viola smiled. Auntie Eliza smiled back.

"Hello, Viola. Florence has told me all about you," she said warmly, climbing out of the carriage. As she did, Viola peered into the coach to see Flo standing there. Her chocolate brown hair was tied up in a plait held together by a red ribbon. Her green eyes were as bright as they always were, and a big grin was plastered across her freckled face.

"Viola!" she cried, racing out of the coach. She grabbed Viola and pulled her in for the longest hug.

"Welcome home," Viola smiled. She was desperate to tell Flo all about the Emerald Lady and Walpole, the thief and his woodland shack - but as she glanced back at her father who raised his eyebrows at her, she knew that meant to remember what he just said.

"Do you want to sit here quietly and watch them groom the horse?" Viola said solemnly, pointing at the carriage. Flo screwed up her nose.

"Good heavens, no!" Flo laughed. "I want to make mud pies and play hide and seek! I've been dreadfully bored on my own in Brighton. I want to have some fun!"

Viola cheered and took her hand, running past Mr Pumpernickel who shook his head with a gentle smile. He was happy that Viola had her friend back, if only for a little while.

"Where are we going?" Flo called as they ran out of Brookwater Lane.

"I have something very special to show you!" Viola beamed.

"Our tree!" Flo cheered happily, looking up at the old oak she used to play in with Viola, Rupert and Teddy, before she went away. They would spend countless hours climbing up and hanging from its many branches. After Flo had moved away, Viola and Teddy had decided to build a proper treehouse in it. Teddy had managed to gather enough scrap wood from various places to build it. It took him many weeks to work on it but he believed it was worth all the splinters in his hands and tired, achy muscles.

Teddy was very clever when it came to building things. He had a "real eye for woodwork," according to their father.

It was rather small and didn't have many fancy features, but it had a rope ladder, a little window, a floor and a roof. It was a marvellous secret hideout for them to play in. Viola had added an old blanket and a cushion that Mrs Pumpernickel had kindly donated to make it cosy. She had taken shelter in there one stormy afternoon with Rupert and Teddy and the treehouse did its job in keeping them dry.

Viola and Flo sat in the treehouse, dangling their legs over the rope ladder. It offered a beautiful view of the lavender filled Hyde Park and Kensington Gardens from one side and the other overlooked the less picturesque industrial heart of London. A huge, disused iron foundry stood menacingly in the centre, surrounded by smaller grey factories and other such foreboding buildings. It had been the site of many a game of hide and seek, and Viola knew the layout of balconies, gantries and old machinery like the back of her hand, having had many exciting adventures in there. As exciting as it was, however, it was also rather terrifying. Rumour had it that the ghost of the former night watchman, Eli Silversmith, would haunt the grounds, looking for children to catch. Understandably, that was enough to ensure they never went in there after dark. Besides, there was always a policeman or two checking that vagrants hadn't got in and set up home. Viola had lost count of how many times they'd been told off for "messing around" in there by the police.

Watching a mother bird build a nest for her babies in one of the upper branches, Flo turned to Viola.

"I've missed you," she said quietly. "It hasn't been much fun since I left London. Sometimes I feel guilty whenever I want to laugh or smile or even feel happy because Father has died and poor mother is in hospital."

"You must still enjoy your life, Flo. You can't feel sad all the time. Every day you must find something that makes you smile." Viola felt a little silly saying such things, being lucky enough to have both parents alive and well, but she didn't know what else to say to make Flo feel better. After all, Viola had no idea just how terrible it was.

"When Father died, I was so furious. I saw people going about their lives and it made me angry. How could they continue when something so terrible had happened? My life had changed in seconds but everything else was the same as it was. It was the same, but different. Does that make sense?" Flo asked. Viola nodded; she remembered what it was like when her grandfather died. It was a warm summer's day and her mother was sobbing in the kitchen. Her father had gathered her and her brothers in the front room to tell them. Viola felt that somebody had slowed down time and the sadness seemed endless. Her father had told them to go outside and play to cheer themselves up, but none of them wanted to. They would just stand in the street in silence, unsure of what to do with the overwhelming sense of grief. Shortly after his funeral, Mrs Pumpernickel gave Viola her father's old pocket watch. It had helped Viola to learn how to tell the time and she kept it with her, even after the watch stopped working. They all missed Grandfather Edmund greatly. Even now, Viola still hears her mother crying sometimes when she doesn't think anyone can hear her.

Flo's Aunt and Uncle were both very loving and kind and Flo couldn't have asked for better people to care for her in her mother's absence. Auntie Eliza was married to a judge called James who was very wealthy. They lived in a big house with a big garden and even had people working in the home to look after them. Flo's mother, Emily, was Auntie Eliza's sister and was now in a very nice hospital that Eliza and James paid for. Apparently, she was well cared for by the doctors and nurses there and her room overlooked a beautiful garden. Eliza tried to visit Emily as much as she could but Flo only came down to London once in a while. She was at a school in Brighton which was something that Viola had wanted to do for such a long time. As Viola's parents weren't wealthy, they couldn't afford a proper school and so Viola never went. Her mother said that she would learn everything she needed in life by working in the shop and helping around the house. They would sit down together and work on reading and writing, cooking and cleaning and Mr Pumpernickel would teach her about numbers and money in the shop. Viola used to agree that learning in the house was the best thing, but having heard Flo's wonderful stories of her school friends and all the fascinating things she had learnt, she wished she went to one.

Flo's clothes looked different too. Before her mother became ill, Flo's clothes were like Viola's - a little shabby and either too big or too small for her tiny body. Now, they were made of very fine fabrics and looked truly beautiful. Her shoes were so shiny that they would glisten in the sunlight. Viola's shoes were clean enough but they rarely sparkled.

"Let's go and play some games and then we can have some of your mother's scrummy sponge cake," Flo announced, having grown bored of the static house in the tree. Viola frowned.

"My father didn't think you'd want to play. He thought you might be a little too sad," Viola said carefully. Flo laughed.

"Of course, I want to play! Come on, I'll race you." Before Viola could object or tell Flo about her episode with Plumb, Flo was gone, climbing down the many, many rungs of the ladder.

As they passed Wilton's Theatre on their way home to the bakery, a huge eruption of applause escaped through a small open window. Flo stopped and looked up.

"What's that?" she asked, turning back to Viola.

"Ruby Dancer," Viola smiled, telling Flo all about the poster she and Rupert had seen and the round man that was trying to coax people into the theatre to see her. She also told her that these places were not suitable for children. Flo shrugged.

"Think of all the fun they are having inside. It sounds wonderful," she said as another round of applause poured out. Viola nodded.

"Look," she said, just as the stage door flung open. A man who looked suspiciously like the grocer, old Mr Granger, fell out. There was a larger man behind him, smoking a cigarette.

"Go home, Alf," the man from the theatre yelled, before throwing a coat on top of him. The man looked incredibly angry but Mr Granger, however, seemed to be having a whale of a time. He raised a hand as if to say sorry but soon began laughing like a little boy. The man rolled his eyes, turned around and went back into the theatre, letting the door slowly swing shut behind him.

"Quick!" Viola whispered, grabbing Flo's arm and pulling her towards the door, kicking her leg in the doorway to stop it closing.

"We can't!" Flo giggled, covering her mouth. Viola smiled back.

"You said it yourself - think how much fun it is in there!"

# Chapter Ten
## The Magic of Theatre

With a creak, the door closed behind them. As it did so, a dreadful stench of old ale and musty tobacco filled their nostrils. It was so horrid that Viola felt quite nauseous. Flo turned to her and covered her nose – she obviously disliked it too. The foyer of the theatre was dark and smoky and the din of the audience could be heard from further within. As they walked slowly towards a door marked 'Auditorium,' Flo squeezed Viola's hand. They weren't going to be separated for anything.

"Ready?" Flo asked, reaching the door. "We mustn't get caught. Auntie Eliza would be very disappointed in me." Viola nodded in agreement. Her parents would be rather annoyed too.

Flo pushed the door open and the noise hit them like a steam train. A great swarm of people sat around circular tables, each covered in a dark red cloth, drinking whiskey and ale. The overpowering smell of alcohol and tobacco was even stronger than before. Flo had decided she wanted to leave then and there. She turned to Viola to tell her to go when the theatre suddenly plunged into darkness. The audience fell silent with anticipation as a spotlight lit up a woman standing in the centre of the stage.

It was Ruby Dancer.

She was wearing a beautiful, red dress that seemed to sweep as she danced. The music was so loud and powerful that it made Viola want to dance right there on the spot. The girls stood watching, spellbound for a few moments, absolutely transfixed by the beautiful dancing and vibrant music. The audience seemed enthralled too – they watched in awe as Ruby elegantly pirouetted round the stage, moving in a way so beautiful and effortless that it didn't seem possible. As the music slowly came to an end, Ruby moved to the centre of the stage and suddenly started to float. She lifted off the stage and high into the air, spinning round and round, up and down, arms stretched out. She looked like she was swimming in mid-air. The audience erupted with cheers and applause, rising to their feet.

"She's flying!" Flo whispered. "It's magic!" She pointed to Ruby who was still floating in the air. Viola's mind was working quicker than ever before.

*It can't be magic - magic doesn't exist.*

Viola pushed her way through the audience, desperate to get a closer view of the amazing show. Flo called out to her and Viola reached out a hand.

"Come with me!" Viola cried over the cheers of the crowd. Flo grabbed her hand and they made their way through to the stage their presence seemingly ignored by the theatre's patrons. As the curtain slowly fell to signal the end of the show, Viola saw what she was hoping for – through the smallest of gaps in the staging, a man was pulling at a long rope which was connected to a wheel-like contraption above Ruby. The wheel, in turn, was connected to some very thin wire that seemed to go down to Ruby, supporting her in the air. Just as the curtain reached the floor Viola saw, on the other side of the stage, a large weight that sat on the floor, again connected to the wheel by a rope. Viola knew it wasn't magic - it was a simple rope and pulley system.

"That was amazing. She's like a magical angel," Flo gushed, truly amazed by what she had seen. Viola didn't think she would ruin her moment just yet by revealing that it was all just a clever trick.

As the pair returned to the bakery that evening, they walked past the burned-out shop where Jeffers Books once stood. Although still recognisable as a shop, there was no signage or indication as to what it once sold. Viola felt deeply saddened. It was such a beautiful shop but now it was the scene of a nightmare.

Mr Jeffers appeared at her side walking with a stick.

*He never used to have one of those*, Viola thought.

"Miss Pumpernickel," he smiled.

"Good afternoon, Mr Jeffers," she beamed. It was lovely to see him again.

"Will you reopen the shop soon, Mr Jeffers?" Flo asked hopefully. He took a few seconds before he replied.

"I won't be reopening at all, I'm afraid." The girls gasped. "I can't afford to. But I have been assured that a new book shop will be here soon enough."

"What do you mean?" Viola asked, confused. If he wasn't opening the book shop, who was?

"I'm an old man, girls. I simply don't have the energy to rebuild the shop following the fire. Collicott Law has very kindly bought it from me and will do what it takes to make it great again. It's not worth much in its current state but they have been very generous in their offer. I'll rent out a small room somewhere and live out my retirement quietly." He was sombre and Viola noticed the twinkle in his eyes had vanished.

"But Mr Collicott is a solicitor. He doesn't know anything about books," Flo exclaimed.

"But *you* do," Viola added. "You're the best bookseller in London. You can't give up."

"Thank you, but I'm afraid it's already done. I'm just happy I got out of that fire alive," he sighed, tapping Viola on the shoulder. "I wouldn't be here without you. I owe you my life."

"How much further?" Flo asked with a sigh, the following morning. The basket of fruit and bread was starting to hurt her arm. Viola stopped.

"Just another road or two. Here, let's swap," she said, handing over two large bottles of broth. One of Mr Pumpernickel's regular customers, Mr Johnson, had been poorly for quite some time and so, feeling that he needed a little pick-me-up, Mary and Albert had put together a basket of treats including freshly baked bread and fruit from the courtyard. Mary had even made a batch of her famous bug busting broth which promised to banish any nasty germs. She had made it from various bits of fruit and a dash of rum, plus a few other secret ingredients that I couldn't possible divulge to you here and now, but it really did the trick. The downside, of course, was that it smelt revolting and tasted even worse.

Mr Johnson lived alone so Albert had asked the girls to deliver it to him instead. They had been walking a fair distance and, understandably, Flo was getting tired. She wasn't used to walking this far anymore. Her Aunt and Uncle always arranged transport for her in Brighton, so she hardly walked anywhere these days.

"No, I'm sure I can carry on a little further," Flo said with a sigh. She didn't want to admit that she was struggling that much. Viola shrugged and said that if she changed her mind, she would happily take over. As they continued their walk, Viola suddenly stopped.

"Oh no," she whispered, seeing three boys appear from around a corner just ahead. Viola knew them well – and knew they were looking to cause trouble.

"Well, well, well. If it isn't little Viola Pumpernickel," Digby Travers said with a snarl.

"Hello, Digby," Viola rolled her eyes. He was the last person she wanted to see.

"Where you off to, then?" he said, smiling at his two cronies either side of him, Charlie Jackson and Ernie Black.

"Where we go is none of your business," Flo huffed.

"Florence Bramble? Well, I never. I thought you'd run away to the seaside to live the fancy life. We all thought you'd forget about London...and Viola," Digby smiled, his friends laughed too, even though neither of them found him particularly funny.

"Excuse me, we have a delivery to make," Viola said, trying to find a way past the three boys.

"What's the rush? Aren't you going to share some of that lovely bread your father makes with us?" he smirked, shoving his hand into the basket. Flo tried to pull it away but she wasn't quick enough.

"Put that back!" she cried. Digby snorted.

"Or what?" Charlie laughed.

"Yuck!" Digby spluttered, taking a bite of the bread and spitting it to the floor. "Your father couldn't make decent bread if his life depended on it! Everybody knows that!" he laughed, throwing the rest of the loaf into a puddle. He reached into the basket once again and pulled out a lovely, red, juicy apple and bit into it with a crunch. The sap ran down his chin and he wiped it with his sleeve.

"It's so dry," he lied, throwing the apple over his shoulder and onto the floor.

"Leave us alone! I'm warning you. I will tell Teddy," Viola said, her blood boiling. The boys looked at each other and exploded into laughter.

"We ain't scared of him! He's nothing but a goody-goody baker's assistant!" Digby moved closed to the pair. "You heard about them robberies? I wouldn't be surprised if your bakery was hit next - no one is safe apparently. Especially do-gooders," he laughed. His friends stayed silent until he glared at them and they immediately joined in the laughter.

"Are you threatening us, Digby?" Viola asked shocked.

*Could he be involved in the burglaries?*

Digby shrugged.

"It would be awful if your father woke up to find his precious shop empty. Or worse, on fire and you were all trapped upstairs."

He grabbed the bottle of broth from Viola and popped the cork out. He took a huge slug and offered it to his friends who eagerly obliged.

"This ale is disgusting," Ernie said, scowling as he swallowed the thick concoction.

"It's not ale," Viola said quietly. She turned to Flo and raised her eyebrow. "It's poison."

The boys froze.

"W-what?" Digby spluttered. Viola sighed.

"Poison. My mother gave it to me for Father Kelly at the church. They are overrun with rats and this has never failed to kill everything that drinks it."

"You're lying. She's lying!" Ernie panicked.

"She's not! It even killed a horse once. It drank it by accident and next thing you know - dead. Poor thing." Flo did her best to sound convincing.

"Is there an antidote?" Charlie screamed.

"Forget all that, Charlie, how do you *stop* it?" Digby said, tears filling his eyes. Viola tried her best to stifle a laugh. She knew it was wrong to tell such a dreadful lie, but she also knew he deserved it after his many years of cruel bullying.

"Hmmm, let me think." Viola started pacing up and down, enjoying every second. "I seem to remember my mother saying that if you accidentally drink it, or if you drink it on purpose and then regret it, or if you accidently spill it and an animal were to drink it -"

"Yes, yes, get on with it!" Digby yelled.

"You must lie down in a dark room. Don't come outside for many, many days," Flo said slowly.

"And drink lots and lots of milk," Viola added, trying desperately to keep a straight face.

"Ergh! I *hate* milk!" Digby sniffed.

"I know you do, Digby, but it's the only way," Viola sighed. The boys instantly ran off in separate directions, all heading to their homes. Once they knew they were gone, the girls burst into laughter.

"That'll teach them!" Viola said, tears running down her cheeks.

"Come along, we must get to Mr Johnson!"

# Chapter Eleven
### *The Sinister Stranger*

Her heart was thundering through her chest. Never in her life had Viola felt a rush of adrenaline like this. She ran through the dense woodland, which was still recovering from last night's rainstorm, as the twigs and leaves squelched under her boots. She knew these woods well, so could dodge the rogue branches and negotiate the creek that always seemed to appear as if from nowhere. Without stopping to consider what lay before her, she leapt over the thick murky water, using a huge rock as a bridge, and landed on the grass verge with a thud. She turned to look at the figure that was chasing her.

*He's catching me up.*

She took a breath and continued her run, twisting and turning round the fast approaching trees, her legs burning from the intense speed being forced upon them. Viola jumped over the old, fallen tree that had been there longer than she had been on earth and crouched in the shallow pit that she had become so familiar with over the years. A few seconds of still followed, the only sound being her breath escaping her bruised, tired body. She tried with all her might to hold it in so as not to give away her position. She closed her eyes and listened for the footsteps that were closing in. The figure jumped over the fallen tree and landed just feet away from her hideout. Frozen with nerves, she watched as he moved cautiously forward a few steps, trying to decide which way she could have gone.

*I've confused him,* she thought to herself. *This is my chance.*

Slowly she stood, stealthily reaching into her pocket for her missile. She silently placed it in her homemade catapult. Gripping it firmly, she took aim, holding her breath in a vague attempt to steady her shaky arm. Silent calm filled the air as she homed in on her prey. As she finally launched her missile, it felt like an eternity before it reached its target.

*Splat!*

The figure screamed out in frustration, grabbing his back.

"Yes!" Viola boomed, making her presence very much known. "I win again! I make that two nil!" she smiled. Teddy frantically tried to reach the spot on his back where his sister had hit him. A rustling noise made the pair glance over to the thick oak tree standing to their left as Rupert appeared from behind it. He rolled his eyes and picked at the dried egg stain on his shirt. He wasn't very good at these games, unlike his older brother and sister. Even Flo was better than Rupert and she'd never played Egg Tag before. He stopped as he saw something shining amongst the wet grass and bent down to pick it up.

He gasped as he looked at Viola.

"You dropped grandfather's watch," Teddy said, taking the watch from Rupert and handing it to his sister. "You need to keep a better eye on this, Viola."

"Thank you. I didn't know I had dropped it," Viola gasped. She would be distraught if she were to lose that.

"We'd better get home, Mother will be worried," Teddy sighed. When Viola was younger, he would often let her win games to make her feel better but he'd stopped doing that a while ago and he was starting to sulk.

*How can my little sister be so much better at this game than me? I invented it!*

"You don't want to play another game then, Teddy?" Flo laughed, emerging from her hideout behind a tree. She waved two eggs in the air, proving she was still well armed for another round. Teddy shook his head.

"No, my clothes are filthy enough. We'll let you have this one, won't we, Rupe?" He nudged his little brother who nodded.

"How about a race?" Viola said with a smile. Teddy's eyebrows lifted.

"You'd never beat me in a foot race, Viola," he said crossing his arms. "Never in a million years."

Viola sighed, pretending to agree with him. Suddenly, she turned on her heel and raced back into the woodland, heading for home. Caught off guard, Teddy cried out that Viola was cheating. He quickly made his way after her, all the while telling her she was a crook. Rupert's face lit up and he too made his way after the pair. He may not be good at Egg Tag but he was a very good runner.

"I can't run anymore!" Flo cried out. "My legs are exhausted," she laughed. She put the eggs she had been holding into her pockets and started to follow Viola and Teddy. It was nice to have a bit of peace in the beautiful woodland. As she made her way back towards the creek, she stopped to look at the most stunning butterfly that was perched on the trunk of a tree.

A crack of a twig made her spin round.

"Hello?" she called, suddenly feeling that there was somebody behind her.

*Silence.*

Realising that the Pumpernickels had vanished into the distance, she decided she had better get going. It would be dark soon and she didn't have her lamp. She continued her walk, hugging her arms to keep warm. The air was starting to cool. As she turned right at the fallen tree, she stopped.

A man stood in her path.

"All alone?" the man sneered. Flo gulped.

"No, I'm with my friends...they are just over there," she said, pointing in the vague direction that Viola went.

"You'll be wanting to join 'em, no doubt?" he asked. Flo nodded.

"Yes. Excuse me," she said, trying to sound tough.

"What do you know about the robberies in Brookwater

Lane?" he asked with a snarl. He was easily seven-foot tall and was as broad as a horse's carriage. His nose looked as if it had been broken several times and he had an angry, red scar on his face. His voice was deep and scratchy. A rather terrifying figure, really.

"I don't know what you're talking about, sir," she lied.

"Funny that." He took a step towards her. "See, I've 'eard that you've been snoopin' around tryin' to solve these crimes. You ain't a copper - you ain't nothin'."

"Let me pass -"

"I'm warning you, end your investigation or we will end you, Pumpernickel."

"Pumpernickel?" Flo repeated. The man raised an eyebrow.

"That is your name, ain't it?" he snapped.

Flo nodded, shaken to the core.

"Yes...yes, I'm a Pumpernickel," she gulped. She figured it would probably be better to agree with him rather than risk telling him he'd made a mistake. He didn't seem like the type of person to apologise.

"The Governor ain't impressed that you're stickin' your nose in his business. If I were you, I'd leave it alone."

"The Governor?" Flo asked, confused by this new name. The man scoffed.

"Don't act like you don't know who I'm talkin' about. He's the boss and he don't like nosey little oiks like you and your gypsy friend pokin' around his business," he scoffed. "You see this scar? That's his handiwork. I dared to question 'im and he lashed out. He's a nasty brute and he don't like being watched. Leave it alone, girl. He won't warn you again. Understand?"

"Yes, I understand," Flo nodded, as he let go of her shoulder. Once she was free from his grip, she ran out of the woods and headed for the bakery, as fast as her legs would carry her.


"I *could*..." Bertha said when Viola asked her to teach her tarot cards, that evening. They sat on the step of the bakery, watching as the various businesses closed for the night. "But if I did, how would I ever make my money? Everybody would rather go to you for their readings than me!" Bertha teased, giving Viola a nudge on the shoulder. Viola giggled and shrugged. "One day I will teach you, my girl. I'll teach you all about the tarot cards and palm readin' and all the other magical things."

"I don't believe in magic," Viola said bluntly. "Magic is for children."

"All my eye!" Bertha gasped. "Don't talk such hornswoggle! Magic is all around us, little one."

"Not *real* magic though," Viola scoffed.

"Magic is whatever you want it to be. Look at the beautiful star filled sky above us – I'd say that was rather magical, wouldn't you? The beautiful, green grass? Magical. Your brilliant mind? Magic."

"Really?" Viola asked, surprised.

"Oh yes. You'll soon realise that your magical power is to help others. Everybody needs a bit of magic, after all."

"Even you?" Viola asked.

"*Especially* me." Bertha replied with a sigh. Suddenly, Flo burst through the market, rushing towards the pair. Her cheeks were flushed and her eyes looked red and sore. She'd obviously been crying.

"Viola?" Flo gasped. "Viola!"

"What is it?" Bertha asked, sensing something awful had happened. Flo tried to speak but her breathing was short and rapid. Bertha sat her on the step and told her to calm down. "What's happened, sweetheart?" she asked, stroking Flo's hair.

"I was in the woods, walking home after the game, when this man appeared out of nowhere. He thought I was Viola and he told me to stop looking into the Brookwater Lane robberies." Tears were in her eyes.

"How terrifying," Viola gasped. "Did he hurt you?"

"No, no," Flo shook her head.

"What did he look like, this rogue?" Bertha asked concerned.

"He was as tall as the trees with a horrible scar on his chin. He was the most terrifying man I have ever seen," Flo sniffed. Bertha sighed knowingly.

"That sounds like Weston Crabtree. He's a nasty villain known to associate with George Plumb. I've heard some truly vicious stories about him."

"I have never been so afraid in all of my life," Flo whimpered. Bertha bit her lip.

"I'm not having this!" she suddenly bellowed, standing. "This is Plumb's doing. I'm going to tell 'im to leave you both alone. No one threatens my girls and gets away with it!"

Flo took hold of Bertha's hand.

"He told me something else. Apparently, they work for a man called the Governor and he doesn't like that we're looking into the robberies. He's the one who gave Crabtree the scar."

"Oh, my days," Bertha gasped. "I thought he was just a myth. Nobody has ever seen 'im, but we've all heard the 'orrible stories about the elusive Governor. Oh, he's the worst of the worst."

"Does that mean it's over? We can't possibly continue trying to solve the crime if he's that dangerous," Flo said. Viola shook her head defiantly.

"No, we just need to be extra careful. It's high time this Governor was brought to justice."

# Chapter Twelve
## Operation Treehouse

"Here," said Bertha, handing the girls a cup full of steaming hot tea each. "Get these in your gigglemugs." Flo and Viola thanked her as they cupped their hands around the warm beakers; it was chilly up in the treehouse. Bertha had prepared the warm tea at home and brought it in her bag in an old ale bottle. She carried it with her "for emergencies" apparently.

"Why are we here?" Flo asked.

"What happened to you this afternoon, Flo, is terrible. I cannot risk any harm coming to either of you, I would never forgive m'self. The Governor knows we're onto him and he's obviously scared of what we'll find. We must be careful, he's a madman. We must come up with a plan of attack," Bertha said, reaching into her bag and pulling out a large ball of emerald wool and two wooden needles. She started knitting frantically. She noticed the girls staring oddly at her.

"I knit when I'm nervous."

"Our first port of call is Plumb's cabin," said Viola, pacing the floor. "Flo and I will wait until we know he's not around and head back there to see if we can find any clues about the robberies or this mysterious Governor. Secondly, Bertha could ask around at the White Bear pub, I understand Plumb visits there quite a lot."

"No more than I do," Bertha said, before realising that was probably every other night.

"Lastly, Teddy could go to the docklands and see if anyone there knows about him. If that's where Plumb goes to sell what he steals, somebody *must* have heard of the Governor," Viola said.

"But Teddy doesn't want anything to do with it. And he made you promise to not see Bertha anymore," Flo said worriedly.

"Leave my brother to me. I'll get him on side, I promise,"

Needless to say, Teddy was far from impressed when Viola asked him for help. He spent a good while telling her it was a bad idea and explaining just how dangerous it was but Viola didn't give in. If he wanted to stop the crimes that were being committed in their own street, then this was his chance. He finally agreed to help on the basis that she agreed to go straight to the police if he felt they were in danger. Viola agreed, admitting that this was probably a very wise idea.

Bertha, Flo, Teddy and Viola took their places in the treehouse. Teddy had discovered that they could just about make out Plumb's cabin from the top. He had borrowed a pair of binoculars from their father, and was watching the cabin door, waiting for Plumb to emerge. Bertha sat in the corner, still knitting.

They had been over the plan several times and were all set for their investigation into the Governor.

"We have movement," Teddy whispered, as if Plumb could hear him from such a distance. Flo and Viola jumped up, springing into action.

"We'll go to the cabin and see what we can find," Flo said, trying to disguise her nervousness.

"I'll head to the pub," Bertha said, pulling her shawl across her. "Of course, if he comes in I'll have to immerse m'self in the crowd so I'll need a little snifter. All part of the investigation, you understand."

Walpole let out a meaow and curled up in the corner. He knew he wasn't needed for this particular job and was looking forward to a nice cosy sleep. Bertha stuffed her knitting into her bag and stood.

Putting down the binoculars, Teddy turned to face them.

"I'll go to the docklands and see if I can speak to anyone about him. Remember, if we feel we are in danger, we go straight to Constable Clancy, yes? He will protect us," he said, sounding like a captain rallying the troops.

Viola and Flo went down the steps first. Once at the bottom, they ran across the park and towards his cabin, constantly checking that he wasn't making his way back home.

They reached his cabin and took a moment to get their breath back. It was a longer distance than it seemed from the top of the treehouse and Viola regretted suggesting they run the whole way.

Viola knocked on the door and they both hid behind a bush, just in case there was someone else inside. Happy that it was empty, they tried the door. Sure enough, it opened.

"Silly boy, leaving his door open. You'd think a burglar would know better!" Viola laughed as they quickly swooped into the cabin and closed the door behind them. It was tiny inside and crammed full of stuff, far more than when Viola first saw it.

"It smells like a farm," Flo said, turning her nose up. She wasn't wrong, the air smelt damp with the feint scent of horse dung. A wholly unpleasant odour, I can assure you.

Viola began searching high and low, for any clue as to the Governor's identity or what he was plotting. She wasn't sure what she was looking for but felt she would know what it was when she found it.

"There's nothing here," Flo groaned, helping Viola search. Viola agreed with her friend. It was a fruitless search - until she spotted the military jacket thrown carelessly on the floor.

"He was wearing this the night he robbed the watchmakers and butchers," Viola said, picking it up. She shoved her hand into the pockets, pulling out a matchbook, a coin and a scrap of paper. She opened the paper and read aloud the writing scribbled on it:

~~Jeffers Books~~

~~Fletchers Watchmakers~~

~~Barnaby Butchers~~

Haberdashery – nightfall

Pumpernickel Bakery

Tea Shop – protected

Bailey's News – protected

Mr Hawley's Sweet Shop – protected

Aldarich the Apothecarist – protected


All or nothing – A.C.


Viola gasped.

"It's a list of all the shops in Brookwater Lane. He's crossed off the ones he's already robbed. My word, Flo. This is Plumb's hit list!"

"He has the most peculiar writing," Flo said peering over her shoulder. All of the S's are backwards."

"I wonder what A.C. is," Viola whispered, staring at the writing.

"And why does it say that some of them are protected?" Flo added. "What does it mean?"

Suddenly voices from outside filled the cabin, snapping Viola out of her thoughts. Viola thrust the coin and matchbook back into the pocket of the jacket and threw it on the floor in a heap. She stuffed the piece of paper in her apron pocket in a panic.

"Quick! Over here," Viola said, opening a battered wardrobe and throwing herself in. Flo followed, just as the door to the cabin opened.

George Plumb entered the cabin first, followed by another man. The wardrobe door was open just enough to make out Plumb but his acquaintance was blocked from their view.

"You will be paid handsomely, Plumb, you have my word," the unknown man said. Viola frowned.

*His voice is familiar.*

"How handsomely?" Plumb said, slumping in a chair. Viola's heart was throbbing with fear. If he caught them there, it would certainly be game over.

"Enough money to eat for a week. You wouldn't have to beg and borrow," the man said. Plumb thought about it for a moment.

"When and where?"

"The grocers in Honeycomb Walk, just off Brookwater Lane, tomorrow night. The owner, Mr Granger is away visiting his sister and so the shop is being run by his son. He's as lazy and as stupid as a stick. You won't be disturbed."

"Fine. But I want payin' half now and half when it's done," Plumb said. The man agreed and held out a small leather bag. Viola gasped, seeing the man for the first time. It was Digby Travers!

*Was he in on the robberies?*

"I had a feeling you would say that," Digby said, dropping the bag on the table. "Don't spend it all at once," he sneered. Plumb grabbed the bag and pulled it open, studying the contents. Happy the money was correct, he put it back on the table.

"Don't tell the Governor about this. He 'ates me doing jobs on the side. He'd lock me up in the foundry and I'd never see daylight again," Plumb gulped. Digby rolled his eyes.

"Don't worry, I'm very good at keeping secrets."

"Fancy an ale?" Plumb said, pointing to the manky bottle. Digby shook his head, visibly disgusted by the state of it.

Suddenly, Flo's foot slipped and she fell slightly backwards, causing the wardrobe to creak. Both men looked over at it as Viola grabbed Flo to stop her slipping again. Their hearts thundered in their chests.

*Please don't find us, please don't find us.*

"Did you hear that?" Plumb asked, with a frown. Flo held her breath, gripping Viola's hand as tight as she could. Plumb took a few steps towards the wardrobe until he was just feet away from the girls.

"Sounds like rats. I'll bring my dog over, he'll sort them out. He loves nothing more than catching and killing vermin," Digby smiled.

"You ain't bringin' that mangy mutt in 'ere" he snorted, turning back to face Digby. "Nay, I'll get rid of 'em tomorrow."

They bid their goodbyes to each other and once Digby had gone, Plumb slumped in his chair and let out a belch, a belch so loud it made the girls wince in disgust. He plonked his booted feet on the table in front of him and got comfortable. He wasn't going anywhere...and neither were the girls.

# Chapter Thirteen
## *A Shocking Suspect*

Teddy stood at the dockyard, watching for Plumb, nervously shifting from leg to leg. He had no idea what the Governor looked like and so wasn't too keen on hanging around there any longer than was necessary in case he got wind of him asking questions. He didn't much fancy upsetting the leader of a band of criminals.

"I-a know-a no-a Governor-man," said a dock worker. He was a tiny man with hair as black as coal. He wore a flat, tweed cap but it sat at a rather peculiar angle. It was irritating to Teddy, who liked everything to be in its place, and he was tempted to reach out and straighten it.

The dock worker spoke very little English, however, and Teddy didn't speak whichever language was native to him so he decided to thank him and move on.

So far, nobody else was willing to talk to him. He had asked several men about the Governor but they ignored his questions.

Just as Teddy was about to give up and go back to the treehouse, a giant of a man appeared at his side. The man opened a newspaper and seemed to be suddenly engrossed in whichever article he was reading.

"I understand you've been asking questions about the Governor." He spoke without looking at Teddy.

"Yes, yes, I have," Teddy replied, now interested in this rather peculiar man next to him. "Do you know him?"

"Oh yeah, I know him, alright. I know who he is and I know where he is," the man said firmly. "But it will cost ya."

"How much?" Teddy sighed.

"How much do you have?"

"Three shillings," Teddy lied, knowing he had more than five in his pocket.

"Done," the man said, closing the paper. He looked around before speaking. "The Governor comes here once in a while, patrolling the docklands, making sure we're all doing as we should be, and by that, I mean watching the boats comin' in and sizing up what they're carrying. If it's worth anythin', we'll look a bit further and then, if we like it, we nick it. Then we sell it on and give the money to our boss, the Governor."

"Is he behind the Brookwater Lane robberies?" Teddy asked.

"Course he is. He's behind most of the crimes round 'ere. But he's vicious. He comes across all sweet and kind but if you cross him, you'll regret it," the man said, leaning into Teddy. He noticed he had a rather angry looking scar running down his face.

"And what's his name?" Teddy knew that he was ever so close to finding out this rogue's identity and could barely contain his desperation.

The man looked around before leaning into Teddy.

"You understand this man is dangerous? He's very powerful. You mustn't try and challenge him. Are you sure you want to know? Once I say his name, you can never unhear it."

"Yes, please tell me. He's threatening my sister and I need to keep her safe."

The man folded up the paper and held his hand out for the coins. Teddy obliged and asked him one final time for the Governor's real name.

"Adam Clancy," the man whispered. Teddy was stunned. "He's a policeman, he works down in Whitechapel."

"I-I don't believe you," Teddy stuttered.

"Don't be fooled by the uniform, boy. He's a dangerous villain," the man sniffed. He pointed to the scar on his face. "Who do you think did this to me?"

"It can't be him, he's our friend. He's an officer of the law!"

The man shrugged.

"It's the perfect cover, ain't it? Who would suspect the one person supposed to protect us?"

A horrible wave of realisation spread over Teddy. "No wonder he wasn't interested in helping us before. If he is the thief, he wouldn't want us sniffing around, would he?"

The man glanced behind him, worriedly. Teddy noticed a couple of police constables chatting to a dock worker just a few feet away.

"I've said too much," the man whispered before walking away from Teddy.

"Wait! Who are you?" Teddy cried as the man vanished into the crowd.

Bertha reached the treehouse first. She had been waiting for just a short while when Teddy arrived. Bertha hardly let Teddy climb up the ladder before she spoke.

"I sat in that awful pub for hours and nobody knew anythin' about the Governor. They all looked at me as if I'd sprouted horns."

Teddy slumped against the wall of the treehouse, still reeling from his discovery. Bertha, for the first time, noticed that he was as white as a sheet.

"You alright, sweetheart?"

"Nobody had heard of the Governor at the docklands either, or if they had, they certainly weren't telling me. And then, just as I was about to give up, a man appeared. He told me who the Governor is."

"Edward Pumpernickel, you little diamond! Who is it?"

Teddy took a deep breath, unable to believe he was about to utter the words.

"Constable Clancy."

"We can't go to 'im, he never believes a word I say," Bertha said, waving her hand.

"No." Teddy's voice was firm. "Constable Clancy is the Governor." His words stunned her. Silence engulfed them, as Bertha took in what Teddy had said. After a moment, she started to chuckle.

"Surely not! He's a policeman! A very nice policeman at that."

"That's exactly what the man said. He's as nice as pie but then, if you upset him, he turns nasty. I would never have thought it of Mr Clancy."

"Who told you all this? Did you recognise him?"

"No, and he never told me his name. He was rather menacing though, I must say."

"We can't believe the word of a stranger over our friend!" Bertha said. Teddy shrugged.

"Clancy could be hiring Plumb and some other thugs to do the crimes he wouldn't have the stomach to commit himself. Being so well liked, he'd never be suspected. Of course, he could easily place the blame at someone else's door to ensure that he never gets found out," said Teddy. "It's brilliant. Terrible, of course, but brilliant."

"Nay, I refuse to believe it. It just ain't possible," Bertha shook her head. "Your informant was wrong."

Teddy sighed and lay on the floor. He was tired and his head hurt. He closed his eyes and replayed the conversations he'd had at the docks over and over in his head.

"Italian," Bertha said, after a moment.

"Excuse me?" Teddy asked, opening his eyes.

"The dock worker you spoke to earlier, the one with the wonky 'at? He was Italian. You were wondering where he came from," Bertha said with a sniff.

"Good grief, how did you know what I was thinking?"

"Have you learnt nothing, Ted?" she smiled. Teddy raised his eyebrows. For the first time, he was starting to realise that perhaps Bertha Bard did have some supernatural gifts after all.

"Where are the girls?" he asked, suddenly. Bertha jumped up in horror.

"Plumb!" she cried, racing down the ladder.

Flo and Viola had been trapped in the wardrobe for hours. It was probably only one or two but you know how the mind can play tricks on you, especially when you are secretly locked in the home of a potentially dangerous criminal.

They had been too frightened to attempt to whisper so had been trying to communicate by using their hands. Viola tried to tell Flo that they should wait until Plumb falls asleep and then flee, but Flo thought she was talking about swimming so they never really came up with a plan.

Unfortunately, Plumb seemed quite settled for the evening and didn't appear to be heading out any time soon. Viola was getting more and more anxious – they had to get out somehow. She could see through the tiny gap in the door that Plumb was sitting at his table eating some sort of brown slop. It looked utterly vile and the stench was enough to make the girls gag. He seemed to be enjoying it though, washing it down with gulp after gulp of ale, followed by the occasional belch. The girls were feeling positively queasy watching, and hearing, him eat his dinner. He stood and threw the empty bowl into the sink – on top of several other bits of dirty crockery – and slumped in his armchair. He picked at his teeth for a moment, let out one final belch and closed his eyes.

He was having a post-dinner nap, just like Mr Pumpernickel did on a Sunday afternoon. Viola didn't remember her father ever picking his teeth or belching uncontrollably, mind you.

Once his snoring started to fill the cabin, Viola put a finger up to her mouth. Flo nodded and did the same.

Viola pushed open the wardrobe door, which suddenly creaked loudly. The girls froze as they glared over at Plumb who thankfully, seemed oblivious to the noise. They squeezed out of the wardrobe and slowly made their way to the front door, careful to avoid stepping on the many obstacles scattered on the floor. Flo got to the door first and gently turned the handle, looking back at Plumb to make sure he was still sleeping.

"We did it!" Flo whispered with a smile as she pulled open the door unexpectedly revealing Teddy and Bertha standing on the other side. Flo let out a yelp of surprise which caused Plumb to stir. He let out a sleepy moan, shifted position and fell back into his slumber.

"Quick!" Viola whispered, pushing Flo out of the cabin. As the door slammed close behind them, Plumb's eyes opened, wide awake this time.   He jumped out of the chair and rushed to the window, peering from behind the dirty net curtain.

"Someone was 'ere..."

# Chapter Fourteen
*The Raven Dog Catcher*

After her scary encounter with the stranger in the woods and being trapped in Plumb's cabin, Flo had decided to spend the following day at the hospital with her mother. It was much safer. Not as much fun, of course, but safer.

Teddy and Bertha had told the girls about their suspect, Constable Clancy, which deeply upset Viola. She cared a great deal for Clancy – could he really be the villain? She felt the same as Bertha – it wasn't him. Teddy's information was wrong. It *had* to be.

Viola found herself sitting outside Pumpernickel Bakery on her own, waiting for something fun to happen to distract her from their investigation. She was rarely disappointed – the streets of Brookwater Lane held much entertainment for Viola: market traders shouting and hollering, policeman chasing wayward lads through the crowds and, on occasion, grown men being thrown out of the White Bear pub for, what Viola could only assume was being a bit too cheeky.

Today was different, however.

The sky was purple black and the air was cold – so cold that people didn't want to stop and chat at the market stalls, and the naughty lads obviously chose to stay at home rather than cause any trouble outside in the bitter cold. Bertha had suggested that they all "get back to normal" for a while so as not to arouse any suspicion, but she promised she would continue devising a plan to expose the Governor.

Viola was about to give up and go inside to play with Rupert when she saw something that made her insides freeze with fear.

The Raven Dog Catcher was heading towards the bakery, carrying an empty sack over his shoulder. He stopped every now and again, checking under barrels and down alleyways, obviously looking for any stray dogs he could scoop up. Viola got up from the step and watched in silent fury as he continued his search.

Viola's fists were clenched so tightly that her arms were shaking with anger. She could feel the blood rushing through every vein in her body. She frantically scanned the street, desperate for something – anything - that could help her stop this awful man once and for all. Bundled up underneath the stall nearest to her, she saw a huge pile of netting. Grabbing a corner, she cried out for Teddy who rushed out of the shop at her call.

"Viola? What on earth?"

"There's no time, Teddy. Please help me!" she pleaded. Realising how desperate his sister was, he grabbed the other end.

"What now?" he asked.

"Climb as high as you can. We must trap him." Viola had

already started ascending the barrels and window sills until she reached a small ledge above the fish stall. The stench was utterly dreadful but for once, she didn't care. This was far more important.

"Now what do we do?" Teddy asked, standing on the upper level of the bank opposite.

"Now, we wait."

After a few moments, the Raven Dog Catcher approached. The market-traders and their customers hadn't noticed the two children above them, they were far too busy trying to haggle the best deal and get out of the cold.

"Him," Viola hissed, pointing to the man making his way toward them. He was still carrying his ever-present grey sack over his shoulder. However, there now seemed to be something heavy wriggling inside it.

Viola's heart sank.

*He has stolen another poor dog.*

With every step, the man grew closer and closer to their trap. He was so close that Viola could hear him whistling over the din of the market. Teddy looked at his sister, eyes wide. Viola shook her head. He wasn't in position yet.

*Just a few steps more...*

The Dog Catcher was now standing directly beneath them.

Viola signalled to Teddy to drop the netting. He nodded and went to release his grip. Suddenly, Viola shook her head frantically, pulling as hard as she could on the net. The Dog Catcher had double-backed to the chestnut stall on the other side of the fishmongers and was chatting with the stall holder.

In the confusion, Teddy had lost his footing and slipped. He reached out, fearing that he would plummet down the two storeys to the pavement, letting out a cry of desperation, causing the Dog Catcher to look around, curious at the strange sound. Teddy somehow managed to save himself by grabbing a brick jutting out of the wall. Still holding the netting, he scrambled to find a safe footing. Eventually, he was back in position, but his heart was beating double quick.

Within seconds, the Dog Catcher had finished his conversation with the chestnut seller and moved right into their trap.

"NOW!" Viola screamed, releasing the net. Teddy obeyed and dropped the end he was holding. The man cried out as the heavy netting engulfed him. Several passers-by rushed to his aid but Viola and Teddy had already clambered their way down in time to stop them.

"Stop! Don't help him!" Viola cried. "He steals dogs and kills them!"

The crowd gasped in horror.

"No, I don't!" the man yelled, desperately trying to escape his prison. Teddy grabbed the sack and pulled it open. A small, black dog poked its head out, revealing a rather nasty and sore looking eye.

"See? Lord knows what he had planned for this poor soul," Teddy announced to the shocked audience gathered around them.

"Someone find a policeman! Arrest him!" said a woman from the crowd.

"It ain't true! I promise ya!" the man said. The dog's unwell and I'm taking 'er away to fix 'er."

"Don't talk such hornswoggle," Viola snapped, folding her arms across her chest.

"Just let me out and I'll show ya," the man said, tugging at the netting. Viola laughed sharply, signalling that wasn't going to happen.

As the battle of wills continued, the crowd seemed split on whether to believe the man or not, with cries resonating through the street of "Set him free!" and "Lock him up!"

"We cannot trust the word of a child!" boomed a male voice from deep within the mob. Viola was speechless; why wouldn't they believe her? Surely her age wasn't a factor on whether the truth was being told or not?

"Look!" the Dog Catcher cried. "She'll tell ya. She'll tell ya I'm innocent." He pointed towards the crowd at a woman struggling to make her way to the front. The people slowly parted to reveal the Emerald Lady. Viola's face lit up with relief.

"Bertha! We've caught the Raven Dog Catcher – tell them how awful he is!" she beamed, rushing to her side. Instead of sharing her joy, Bertha frowned.

"Viola, what have you done?" she asked softly.

"Tell them," Viola repeated, tears filling her eyes. She couldn't understand why Bertha wasn't beside herself with joy. She loved animals just as much as Viola did.

"Let him go," Bertha said, turning to the crowd. Two burly men pushed past Viola and pulled the netting off the man and the poor cowering dog. Viola tried to stop them by grabbing the netting but Bertha pulled her back. "Leave it, Viola. Let this man go."

Viola looked at Teddy who was helpless to stop them. He knew he couldn't keep this man trapped any longer. Of course, he would have gone to fetch Constable Clancy, but he didn't know whether he could trust him right now. He reluctantly pulled the heavy netting off the man.

"Alright, alright. Don't you all have better things to be doin'?" Bertha said to the crowd who almost instantly dispersed. Viola's eyes poured tears down her flushed cheeks.

"Why did you help him?" she sobbed, tearing herself away from Bertha's arms. "Why did you let him go when he is so cruel to all those dogs?"

"You need to start talking, Miss Bard." said Teddy firmly. He hated seeing his sister so upset.

"Listen to me, this man ain't hurting the dogs. He's helping 'em. I'll show you, if you trust me." Bertha crouched down to be level with Viola. She looked up at her brother who took a breath. "You do trust me, don't you, Viola?"

"Yes, of course I do but ⸓"

"Then let me prove to you that he's a good man."

"Very well," Teddy replied for Viola, taking her little hand in his. "But I'm coming too."

The Dog Catcher and Bertha led Viola and Teddy to a boarded-up shop through the other side of Cobble Lane alley. The

Pumpernickels had walked past it numerous times without giving it a second glance until now. The Dog Catcher pulled back the corner of a board covering the doorway and beckoned them in. Once inside, he lit a candle and handed it to Bertha. He lit a second one for himself. There was just enough light to make out a large table in the centre of the room with lots of bottles and jars running along it. There were piles of bandages and wooden splints in an open box sitting on the floor.

"That's where I treat 'em," the man said, pointing to the table. It wasn't as horrendous as Viola had imagined and surprisingly, it looked rather clean. "Once they've been treated, I let 'em sleep in the den. I give 'em some grub and when they're strong enough, I sell 'em to people what can look after 'em. People what will love 'em, I make sure of that," he sniffed. "I use whatever money I get to buy more medicine, and a bit of food for me, now and again."

Viola peered inside the den to see three dogs fast asleep on a huge pile of blankets. They looked so comfy and cosy that Viola was tempted to curl up alongside them herself. There were several bowls of water and a plate of half eaten sausages which Viola assumed was their lunch.

"The butcher, Mr Barnaby, he gives me scraps for 'em 'cos I helped his terrier a while back. Nice fella," the man said, noticing Viola's interest. "I promise you, I'm telling the truth," he said gently. For the first time, Viola believed him.

"What about this poor dog?" Teddy asked, pointing at the dog that had climbed out of the sack. Her eye still looked incredibly sore. The man crouched down and carefully picked her up, whispering a few soothing words as he did so.

"Here we are," he said, putting her on the table. She didn't seem afraid of him. Viola wondered if she knew that he was helping her. He grabbed one of the jars and poured some white liquid onto a strip of bandage. He took some blue powder and scattered it liberally onto the liquid. He slowly and carefully placed the bandage onto her eye. She whimpered slightly but didn't resist. A moment passed and the man removed the pad. Her eye was still red but nowhere near as bad. He nodded and replaced the bandage. He took a longer strip and tied it round and under her chin, securing the pad in place. The dog nuzzled the man who made soft, shushing noises to comfort her.

"She'll get some dinner in her belly and a good night's sleep and I'll check on her tomorrow," he said, stroking her head. Viola scanned the room, looking at the jars and bottles scattered about. Many of them had strange and intriguing names that Viola couldn't possibly pronounce. She picked up a peculiar pink and bubbly liquid, in a long thin tube.

"No, no, don't touch that, little one," the man said, quickly taking it out of her hand. "That's snake venom. Nasty stuff. I extracted that from a cat what was bitten. The little blighter was very poorly but I managed to save 'er. She'll think twice before attacking another viper, I can tell ya!"

Viola nodded and glanced at his hand as he put the bottle back where it was.

"How did you lose your fingers?" she asked. "Did a dog bite you?"

"No, not a dog. I was hit by a runaway horse and carriage when I was a young 'un. It ran over me hand and I lost two fingers. Nay bother, I do without 'em."

Viola smiled awkwardly. She wasn't sure how to respond to such a comment.

"Here. Have some of this, it's Walpole's favourite," the man smiled, handing her a jar of white and green liquid.

"W-what is it?" Viola said suspiciously, looking at the jar.

"Basil milk. It's a little treat for the animals when they're recovering. Animals love the stuff, but it's perfectly safe for us humans. And rather tasty too!"

Viola smiled at the thought of Walpole as he handed glasses of basil milk to Teddy and Bertha, the last of whom downed it in one.

"What's your name, sir?" Viola asked, suddenly.

"People call me Doc."


Bertha found herself wandering through the crowded market on her way home from the makeshift animal clinic. Ordinarily she would walk with her head low to shield her face from those who weren't happy with what she did for a living. They would often shout nasty things and sometimes even push and shove her, so she would hide her face for protection. Today, however, she felt brave. Maybe it was seeing Viola stand up for what she believed in – albeit wrongly, but

Bertha felt courageous enough to hold her head up high for the world to see.

She would stare at every man she walked past, wondering if they were the Governor. She refused to believe that Clancy was behind all the robberies. It just couldn't be true. Teddy's informant must have said it was him to try and throw them off the scent of the real villain. It was too loud and frantic for her to tap into anyone's thoughts so she had to rely on her gut feeling. She stood, scanning the crowd for anyone that appeared extra suspicious but, save for a pickpocket, two drunks and a vagrant, there wasn't anyone that would fit the bill of a criminal mastermind.

Turning into Cobble Lane, Bertha stopped by the boxes she used for her readings and reached into her bag. She pulled out a large leather-bound book and sat on a box, as Walpole sat by her feet. A calm silence enveloped them.

"Are you going to follow me around all afternoon or are you going to actually say somethin'?" she said suddenly, not looking up from her book.

"Good afternoon, Miss Bard," Constable Clancy appeared from the shadows behind her. He walked around the boxes so that they were face to face.

"I ain't doin' nothin' wrong, Clancy. I'm allowed to read me book in peace and quiet."

"You are leading the Pumpernickel children down a dangerous path." He spoke slowly and deliberately. "Why are you so determined to bring them harm?"

Bertha stood up.

"I ain't bringing 'em harm. I'm helping 'em solve the Brookwater Lane robberies, seeing as you refuse to believe anything we have to say!" she cried, deeply insulted that he thought she would encourage someone to hurt them. Especially after what had happened to her daughter, many years ago. Surely he could understand that, being a father himself.

"I hear you've been asking questions in the pub. Teddy too, at the docklands. Tell them all to stand down, Bertha."

"They are very independent children, they won't listen to me," Bertha said casually.

"Stand. Them. Down," he boomed. "If you continue to go down this route, I will have no option but to arrest you."

"Arrest me? For what?"

"I'll think of something. Leave the Pumpernickels alone - they are good people. They don't deserve to get involved in this," he whispered. Bertha gulped.

"You don't scare me, Clancy," she hissed. Clancy took a step closer to her and sniffed sharply.

"If I hear that you, or the Pumpernickels, have been asking any further questions about the robberies, I will lock you up and make sure they lose the key. Do you understand?"

After a second, she nodded. He took a breath and turned away, leaving her alone in the alley.

She slumped on the box, her legs feeling shaky. She knew he was a man of his word. She also knew now that Teddy was right after all - Clancy was the Governor, and he had given them one chance to get away. A chance that Bertha had probably just blown.

# Chapter Fifteen
### The Old Lady of Threadneedle Street

Viola sat on the steps leading up to the Pumpernickel home. The bakery had been closed for a while now and the night was closing in.

Holding the list of shops in her hand, she stared at the names as if that would somehow reveal the identity of the Governor. What did A.C. mean? Was it a secret code? Was it someone's initials? It had been written on both notes now and it was more than a little intriguing.

"Viola? Mama says you should have been in bed ten minutes ago," Teddy said, appearing at her side. Viola nodded. He sat beside her and looked at the note in her hands. "We *will* get to the bottom of all this, you know that, don't you?"

He suddenly grabbed Viola's arm, shushing her as he did so. Two men appeared in the dark street just metres away from them, whispering to each other.

It was George Plumb and Digby Travers.

They watched as Plumb walked to the window of the haberdashery and peered into the darkness within as Digby kept a lookout for any passers-by. Plumb tried the handle of the door but it was locked. He tutted and lifted the collar on his grubby coat over his neck and hunched his shoulders up. He was starting to feel the cold. He reached into his coat pocket and pulled out a matchbook before re-joining Digby. Together, they disappeared into the distance, no doubt plotting something dreadful. Teddy looked at Viola and raised his eyebrows.

"What are they up to, I wonder?" he asked. Viola looked down at the list in her hand and sighed.

"The haberdashery is next on this list. They're planning to rob it soon, I feel sure," she whispered. As they looked back to the shop in question, Viola saw a piece of paper on the floor.

Viola rushed to the paper and picked it up. Teddy caught up with her and peered over at the scribbles. The writing was scratchy and small. It seemed very familiar to Viola.

"It's the same writing as the note we found in Plumb's cabin, the S's are all backwards." She held the two notes next to each other to compare. "He must have dropped it just now."

"Move into the light, Viola. I can't make it out," Teddy whispered, pulling her gently to a lamp on the wall:

The old Lady of Threadneedle Street,

Mr Timms,

open the rear window — we'll do the rest.


A.C.

"How peculiar," Teddy said with a shrug. "What does it all mean?" Viola looked up at her brother.

"I don't know, Teddy, but I think I know someone who will."

Bertha jumped out of bed as the banging on her door woke her from a particularly strange dream about giant squirrels. Ever since her chat with Clancy, she hadn't been feeling that well and was having a little nap to try and sleep away her headache.

*Bang! Bang! Bang!*

She reached for a walking cane that she kept under her bed for protection against maltoolers and the like, and raised it as she made her way to the door.

*Bang! Bang! Bang!*

"Who is it?" she bellowed, trying to sound vaguely threatening.

"It's Viola."

"And Teddy!"

Bertha let out a sigh of relief and dropped the cane down by her side. She grabbed a dressing gown that lay on a chair and wrapped it around herself. She may know the Pumpernickel children reasonably well now but she didn't fancy showing them what she looked like in her bedclothes, thank you very much.

She released the many locks she had fashioned and opened the door. Viola and Teddy burst in, chattering at a rate of knots.

"Slow down, slow down!" Bertha cried, raising her arms. She wasn't prepared for such a rude awakening.

"We have to talk to you," Viola said, breathlessly.

"How did you know where I live?" Bertha rubbed her eyes. She peered through the window, worried that Clancy was watching.

"I noticed that you always have muddy shoes and that you smell of lavender. My father and I walk through this park every week and I remembered that there's always a lot of lavender growing here. I know that gypsies sometimes live in these vardo wagons so I thought I'd give it a try and here you are. It was really rather easy, actually," Viola said simply. Bertha raised her eyebrows and shook her head in disbelief.

"Course it was."

"It's a very beautiful wagon, Bertha," Teddy said genuinely, looking around at the impressive interior.

It was a small, red and yellow wooden wagon with huge spoked wheels. The inside however, seemed far bigger than was possible. The living room and kitchen were very cosy with lots of blankets and cushions scattered about, and truly stunning drapes covered the window. Behind the living area was a ladder that led up to the sleeping quarters which looked like an exceptionally comfortable bed. Far more so than her own tiny bunk bed. In the opposite corner, a birdcage hung from the ceiling. Instead of housing a bird there were several candles, all different sizes, scattered within.

"Well, it's my little home. It ain't much but it's mine," Bertha smiled as Viola looked at a large leather-bound book that sat on the table.

"What a curious book," Viola said, lifting the cover.

"That's me Book of Names. I record every reading I do in there." Bertha gently took the book from Viola and held it to her chest. "You shouldn't be here. You need to get yourselves home."

"We won't stay long Bertha, but we have something to show you," Teddy said, nudging Viola. She pulled the note out of her pocket and handed it to Bertha.

"We saw Plumb and Digby in Brookwater Lane. They were staring at the haberdashery, obviously making plans for their next robbery. This fell out of Plumb's pocket."

Bertha took the note and moved to the light of the oil lamp that sat on the table. She crouched down to read the note properly.

"You're sure Plumb dropped this?" she eventually said.

"Oh yes. Most definitely," Teddy replied. "What does it all mean?"

"The Old Lady of Threadneedle Street- why, that is what some people call the Bank of England," Bertha said, her brain slowly waking up. "Personally, I think it's rather rude. The Bank of England is an important institution and should be regarded as such. Giving it such a silly nickname really boils my cabbage."

"Clancy could be plotting to rob it. He'd be foolish if he is," Teddy laughed bluntly. "They call it The Fortress. I've heard Father talk about it a few times. It has thousands of pounds in its vaults."

"Try millions, boy," Bertha said. Viola gasped.

"Do you know who Mr Timms is or what the A.C. means?" Bertha stood and folded the paper up.

"I can't think straight, I'm still 'alf asleep." She moved to the window and slid the curtain back just enough to peer out. "You weren't followed here, were you?"

"I don't think so, why?" Teddy asked concerned. Bertha proceeded to tell them about the threat Clancy made in Cobble Lane earlier that night and how she knew from experience to believe him when he said he didn't want them asking any more questions about the robberies.

"Constable Clancy wouldn't hurt us," Viola dismissed.

"Please, Viola," Bertha cried. "You don't understand the danger we're in. If Clancy is the Governor, and I'm starting to believe more and more that he is, he will stop at nothing to silence us. You can't be here. You have to go home and forget all about this nonsense."

"No. We are in this together, come what may," Viola said firmly. She moved to the table and started clearing away the plates, cutlery and what-nots that were sitting atop it, much to Bertha's confusion.

"What are you up to?" Teddy asked, equally dismayed.

"I need to plan. I can't think with all this clutter," Viola replied, moving the last plate to the side. She grabbed a chunk of coal from the fireplace and started scribbling on the table.

"Oi, that's me dinner table!" Bertha gasped. Viola shook her head.

"The coal will brush off, I promise," she said, her hand moving quickly across the table. Teddy and Bertha moved closer to Viola, looking at what she had written on the table:

*Robberies - Fires*

*Haberdashery*

*Bank of England*

*Constable Clancy*

*George Plumb*

*Digby Travers*

*Weston Crabtree*

*Mr Timms*

*The Governor*

*A.C.*

Viola took a step back and looked at the table. After a moment, she spoke.

"If we can work out what A.C. means, we're half way there." Viola said, rubbing her coal ridden fingers on her apron. "It could be the name of whoever writes the note?" she said, thinking aloud. Teddy sighed and slumped in a chair.

"My brain hurts, I can't think."

After a moment or two of silence, Viola gasped. Her eyes were wide and her jaw dropped.

"Oh dear," she gulped. "I can't believe I didn't see it straight away."

"What is it?" Bertha asked. Viola frowned.

"A.C stands for Adam Clancy."

Suddenly, a loud bang on the door made them all jump.

"Gypsy?" boomed the voice of Clancy through the door.

"Quick! Hide!" Bertha whispered, pushing them towards the wardrobe at the end of the wagon.

"Not another wardrobe!" Viola cried as she was bundled in with Teddy. Making sure it was closed, Bertha grabbed her shawl and threw it over the writing on the table. The bangs on the front door grew louder and louder as Bertha pulled open the door to reveal Clancy looking rather unhappy.

"Evenin', Clancy," she smiled, trying her best to sound normal. Clancy pushed Bertha to one side as he entered the wagon.

"I've been asked to find two missing children, Viola and Teddy Pumpernickel," he said, scanning the room. "I'm assuming that despite my warnings, they're here with you?"

"No, I've been sleeping in me bed," Bertha shrugged, adding a fake yawn for good measure. Clancy nodded, wholly unconvinced by her performance. He took a step into the wagon and looked around. He glanced at the shawl on the table and moved towards it. Bertha's heart pumped as she watched him lift the shawl. Knowing that if he saw the writing underneath, he'd realise they were onto him, Bertha suddenly pushed a chair to the ground. He spun, shocked by the loud noise, dropping the shawl back onto the table.

"Oops, I slipped," she smiled. "Sorry if I made you jump, Adam."

He frowned, curious at her sudden use of his real name.

"I am Constable Clancy to you," he hissed. As he turned to leave, he noticed a small corner of Viola's apron poking through the wardrobe. He glared at Bertha before marching over and pulling open the doors.

"I think it's best you head home, don't you?" he sighed. Viola nodded and climbed out of the wardrobe, followed closely by Teddy. Clancy didn't give them much opportunity to say goodbye as he escorted them out of the wagon. As the door closed behind them, Bertha let out a huge sigh of relief and slumped at the table. She pulled the shawl off and stared at the list as Walpole jumped onto her lap with a cry.

"I know, Walpole. I know. We're in deep trouble now."

# Chapter Sixteen
*Friend or Foe*

"You're both rather quiet tonight," Clancy said as they walked through the park towards Brookwater Lane. Neither Teddy nor Viola had said a word since they left the wagon. A very curious thing for Viola, indeed.

"We're tired, I suppose," Teddy said, glancing sideways at his sister.

"I know you both think that Bertha is a kind lady but she's not as she appears." Clancy stopped walking.

"She's not the only one," Viola said under her breath.

"Pardon?" Clancy asked, turning to her. Her cheeks reddened; she didn't mean to say that out loud.

"As Teddy said, I'm tired, I don't know what I'm saying," she lied. Clancy frowned. This secretive behaviour wasn't normal for her.

"What is the Emerald Lady plotting?" Clancy asked. Neither Teddy nor Viola dared answer. "I have known your parents since long before you were born. Mrs Clancy and I used to spend every

Christmas with you until our twins came along five years ago. I regard you all as family and I would like to think you felt the same way. In all that time, have I ever given you cause to doubt my loyalty to you?" he asked. The Pumpernickels looked at each other, unsure of how to answer. Viola shook her head.

"No, sir," she whispered.

"Then tell me what you're up to," his voice became a little deeper. His eyes seemed to darken as he spoke.

"We are investigating the robberies and fires, sir," Teddy said, trying to stop his voice from squeaking.

"And what have you discovered?" Clancy asked, crouching to be level with Viola.

"Mr Plumb, Digby Travers and Mr Crabtree have something to do with it, and they all work for a man called the Governor." Viola's voice trembled as she said the final word. Clancy stood.

"I am telling you, in no uncertain terms, do not continue with your so-called investigation. This will bring nothing but trouble your way. Do you hear me?" Clancy asked, firmly.

*Our discovery has rattled him.*

"We know who the Governor is," Viola said, much to Teddy's horror. He grabbed her arm to try and warn her not to say anymore.

"Oh yes?" Clancy sighed.

"We believe his name begins with the letters A and C." She spoke slowly and deliberately, trying to read his reaction. He rubbed his forehead and sighed.

"Who else have you told about this?" he asked, quietly. Teddy shrugged.

"Nobody," he said, folding his arms. "Just us and Bertha."

"Your parents will be worried sick. I must get you home safe," Clancy said, trying to change the subject. Viola nodded, and quickly made her way out of the park, closely followed by Teddy and Clancy.

No one said another word until they got back to the bakery.

Viola lay in her bed, desperately trying to sleep. Every bone in her body was exhausted but her brain was still whirring like a spinning top. She climbed out of her bed and made her way over to the window, hoping to see Walpole sitting on the windowsill. She wouldn't go outside again, not at night time, but she needed to know that she wasn't the only person in London still awake.

She pulled back the curtain and looked out onto Brookwater Lane. It was still and quiet. Rain gently fell onto the street and looked like little sparks as it bounced off the stone pavement. Feeling her eyes start to get heavy, she went to drop the curtain and return to her bed when she saw Clancy pacing, a few yards down the street. She raised an eyebrow as she moved her head closer to the glass. Within a second or two, George Plumb joined him and they stood next to each other, talking closely. Viola wished, more than anything in that second, to be close enough to hear their conversation. She'd give anything to be a fly sitting on one of their shoulders.

Plumb went to walk away from Clancy but the policeman obviously had other ideas. He grabbed Plumb by the arm and pulled him back. His face was twisted and angry. Plumb pulled his arm away and pushed past him, walking away into the night. Clancy let out a sigh, straightened his jacket and slowly continued his patrol of the street. He stopped outside the haberdashery and peered in.

*What's he up to?*

As Clancy turned away from the ribbon shop, he suddenly looked up at her window, locking eyes with Viola. She let out a yelp of fear and dropped the curtain. She ran and jumped into her bed, throwing the cover over her head, hoping and praying that he didn't come after her.

Bertha had summoned them to meet at the treehouse the following day. Flo was back from visiting her mother and was in much better spirits. Seeing her mother get better and better had cheered Flo up so much that she had almost forgotten about her nasty encounter in the woods. Not entirely, but almost.

Bertha had got to the treehouse with Walpole first. She was sitting in the corner finishing off the shawl she had been knitting.

"Why the desperate rush?" Viola asked. She had been helping her father close the shop when Walpole appeared at her feet, crying incessantly. She had given him a tummy scratch and realised that there was a note attached to his collar. It was from Bertha, asking her to gather Teddy and Flo and meet at the treehouse as soon as they could. She was concerned by the urgency of the note but glad for a reason to get away from Brookwater Lane. She wasn't looking forward to bumping into Constable Clancy.

Mr Pumpernickel had then asked Teddy to help with a job in the shop that would only take "five minutes." As soon as the job was done, twenty minutes later, the trio raced out of the shop and headed to the hideout.

"I 'ave a confession," Bertha said quietly. "Yesterday, on me way home from seeing Doc, I bumped into Clancy. Ooh, he was raging, he was. He told me in no uncertain terms to stop our investigation and to leave you all alone or I'd end up in jail," she said, sounding angry at herself. "You can imagine how he must be feeling right now, knowing you came to see me last night."

"He can't arrest you! You haven't done anything wrong!" Flo cried. Bertha raised her hand to calm her down.

"We must stop our investigation. It ain't worth it. Clancy will get his comeuppance one day, have no fear."

"I saw him talking with Plumb last night through my window," Viola said quietly. "I don't know what they said but it wasn't very friendly, I can tell you. Clancy seemed to be very angry with Plumb. Oh, and he saw me watching him."

Teddy frowned and wondered why she hadn't told him sooner.

"We have to trust that the police will turn against Clancy and uncover him as the thief that he is. We just have to give them evidence that they can't deny. And right now, it's not safe for us to continue searching for it." Bertha stopped knitting and sighed. She was so tired and wanted nothing more than to sleep.

"So that's it? We simply give up?" Teddy said shocked. Viola shook her head.

"No! We can't give up," she cried.

"I don't want to end up in jail, Viola. I'm sorry, but my life is *my life*, not yours." Bertha said firmly.

"Mr Collicott will get you out, he's a good solicitor. My father knows him well and can ask him to help you," Viola pleaded. Bertha stood and shook her head.

"Forget all about the robberies and forget all about the Governor."

And with that, Bertha packed up her knitting and climbed down from the treehouse. The trio sat in silence, confused by her actions.

"We're not forgetting about it all, are we?" Flo said worriedly. Viola raised an eyebrow.

"Not in the slightest."

# Chapter Seventeen
### *A Desperate Bertha*

Bertha sat in the shadows, watching the ribbon shop intently. She knew it was only a matter of time before Plumb appeared and she was going to be there waiting for him. After she left the treehouse, she had made her way to the White Bear for a quick nightcap before heading home. She was angry at herself for letting Clancy talk them out of the investigation and needed to calm her nerves. As she sat in the pub, pondering whether she could face Viola again after letting her down, she noticed Plumb, Crabtree and Digby chatting closely in the corner. She stood and slowly made her way to the table near them and sat. She picked up a newspaper from an empty table as she passed and held it up to hide her face. They knew who she was and so she couldn't risk being seen.

"The Guv wants me to rob the ribbon shop tomorrow night. He reckons we're being watched, so we must be careful," Plumb said. Digby shifted in his seat.

"Do you really think that is the best idea? Shouldn't you just leave Brookwater Lane alone now?" Digby said. Plumb and Crabtree laughed.

"No, Travers. The Guv wants to rob every shop until there's none left. They've refused our protection, so we make 'em pay. Now are you with us or are you against us?" Plumb sneered.

"With you," sighed Digby.

"I couldn't get information out of the Pumpernickel girl when I spoke to her in the woods. She was so afraid of me," Crabtree laughed. Bertha wanted to launch herself over the table and whack him with the paper, but knew she couldn't blow her cover.

"I'll wait for nightfall. I'll hide in the shadows, and then I'll strike. I'll get in, get as much of that silk as I can carry and I'll be gone. Quick as lightning," Plumb smiled.

Bertha hadn't told another soul of what she'd heard, especially Viola, but she knew she had to act on it. So, she had been sitting in the doorway of the newsagents opposite the ribbon shop for a while, waiting for Plumb. She was going to catch him red-handed, and he would have no choice but to confess to all the robberies and implicate Clancy when he did.

The haberdashery had been closed for hours and the sky was getting darker with every passing moment. She hadn't slept well the previous evening, due to her late-night meeting with the Pumpernickels and her visit to the pub, and she felt weary. Her eyes were so heavy that she rested her head against the wall, just for a moment.

She woke with a jolt. Walpole was sitting on her chest meowing at her. She took a second to realise that she wasn't tucked up safely in her bed but sitting in the damp doorway opposite the ribbon shop. She pushed Walpole gently off her and sat up. She looked over at the haberdashery in horror – there was someone inside.

She stood quickly and rushed over. The window and front door were both intact – he must have got in through the back. She cursed to herself and peered through the window, desperately trying to see if Plumb was still inside. She could see movement but didn't know who it was.

She grabbed her bag and raced behind the shop. Seeing that the back window had been smashed, she took a breath and approached the building carefully. She peered into the darkness but couldn't see anyone. It was eerily quiet and still.

Bertha slowly pushed the door open and took a step in, listening for any sign of Plumb. She held her oil lamp high as she took a step inside. There had most definitely been a robbery: drawers and cupboards were open with their contents pulled out. She could see that the shelf that once housed rolls of fine Indian silk was now empty. That was expensive fabric; if she was a thief, she would have taken it too.

Then she saw him in the distance, rifling through a drawer.

"Oi!" she yelled, making Plumb jump. "George Plumb! What's your game?" she cried, racing towards him and grabbing him by the collar.

"Leave me alone!" Plumb hissed. Determined to catch this villain, she pulled at his clothes to stop him running away. As he fought to get free from her, she slipped and cut her hand on a shard of broken glass. She immediately let go of Plumb and grabbed her bleeding hand, helplessly watching him run out of the shop.

"Come back 'ere," Bertha gasped, breathless from the brawl. She looked down at her hand and winced. She pushed the wound against a handkerchief from her bag to stop the bleeding.

"Do not move," said a voice over Bertha's shoulder. She slowly turned to see Constable Clancy standing behind her. He grabbed her wrists and shackled them in handcuffs.

"No! No!" she protested, pulling her arms away from him.

"Gypsy? You are under arrest."

"Help me!" cried a voice from outside. Viola and Flo were playing cards with her family in their living room to take their minds off no longer being detectives, when they heard the boy yelling from the street below.

"What on earth is all that commotion?" Mary said going to the window. "Oh, it's that dreadful Travers boy. What has he been up to now, I wonder."

Viola jumped to her feet and rushed to the window, peering out onto Brookwater Lane. Sure enough, Digby was pacing the streets, cradling his dog, Sonny, who seemed to be lifeless in his arms. Tears were streaming down his cheeks as he cried out desperately for help. Viola gasped.

"He needs Doc," she said, jumping down from the chair she was standing on to look outside and raced to the front door.

"Who's Doc?" Mary asked confused.

"He's the animal doctor. He used to be the Raven Dog Catcher but he's not actually," Viola said.

"He's not actually what?"

"A dog catcher. Well, he does catch them but he helps them. He can help Digby," Viola said, pulling on her boots.

"Where are you off to?" Albert asked, putting his cards down. He was onto a winner and didn't want to lose yet another game of Whist, but his daughter's strange behaviour was finally getting his attention.

"I have to help Digby and Sonny. He needs Doc, the animal man," Viola said desperately, a little frustrated at their lack of understanding. Teddy looked at Viola with a frown.

"Please, Viola. Leave him be. I'm sure he'll find the help he needs," Mary said, returning to Albert and Teddy at the table. Rupert was already tucked up in bed for the night. "Digby's a rotten boy. Leave him alone."

"I can't. Please, let me try and help him," Viola pleaded.

"I'll go with her," Teddy said, putting his cards down. "I know Doc will help if he can."

Mary let out a sigh but nodded her agreement. Viola thanked her older brother and they raced down the concrete steps.

"This could be a trap," he whispered to Viola before they reached the bottom. "This could be part of the Governor's plan."

Viola shook her head. "No, he loves Sonny and would never put him in harm's way. Come on, we're wasting time." She turned and raced to Digby, who by now was beside himself with anguish.

"What is it?" Teddy said, looking at Sonny.

"He was run over by a horse. It was running wild, I tell you. Sonny needs help or he will...I can't say the words, it's too awful," Digby choked, tears streaming down his face.

"Doc will help you," Viola said, stroking Sonny's back. Digby had wrapped the poorly dog up in his coat to keep him warm.

"Why should I believe you? You tricked me into thinking I had drunk poison. And you, Teddy. Well, you hate me."

"I don't *hate* you, Digby," Teddy rolled his eyes. "Besides you need our help. You must trust us," he said quietly. Digby sniffed and nodded.

"Please, just help my boy."

They arrived at Doc's clinic less than five minutes later. They banged on the boarded-up door and waited in silence for Doc to answer.

"Yes?" he said, peering round the door.

"Digby's dog was hit by a carriage. Please can you help him? Please?" Viola said quickly. Doc glanced over at Digby and snorted a laugh.

"You?" he said. "You tried to pickpocket me not too long ago. Why should I help you?"

157

"You'll be helping his dog, Sonny. Please?" Viola said.

Doc looked at the dog before frowning and shutting the door with a slam. Digby let out a cry reminiscent of a wounded animal. He looked to the sky and sobbed.

"I'm so sorry, Digby," Viola whispered. "I really thought he would help us."

As she spoke, they heard a clunk and the door opened.

"You'd better come in," Doc said, standing aside and ushering them in.

There was a strange sense of calm within the clinic as Doc took Sonny from Digby's arms and placed him on the table. He checked the dog over, looking in his mouth, his ears, his eyes, his legs and pressing on his tummy. Every now and again the dog would whimper quietly but he didn't have the strength to fight.

"You did the right thing in bringin' him to me. He's in a bad way," Doc said quietly.

"Well, help him then!" Digby snapped. Doc slowly turned to face the lad, shocked at his outburst. "Sorry, I'm sorry. I just want him to be ok. He's my best friend," he sniffed. Viola sighed and looked to the floor.

*Maybe Digby wasn't such a beastly boy after all.*

"He's going to need my full attention. Leave 'im with me overnight and I will do my very best for the little fella."

"Leave him here? You think I'm such a fool as that! I heard you kill dogs," Digby snarled. Doc looked at Viola with a raised eyebrow.

"No, he doesn't, I was wrong," Viola said gently. She was a little ashamed that she had made such a wild, horrid accusation. "He's here to help them. Look," she said, pointing to the den. Digby marched through and peered in, looking at the collection of dogs sleeping soundly. He watched in silence for a moment before returning to the group. He nodded.

"I'll be back in the morning," Digby whispered, kissing Sonny gently on the head. "Thank you, Doc."


As they made their way home after leaving poor Sonny at the clinic, Digby seemed to be in a state of shock. He hated seeing his best friend in such a condition. The emotional turmoil of getting him the medical help he needed had taken its toll.

"I don't know how to thank you," Digby said quietly. "You saved Sonny. I owe you everything."

"Don't be silly, we couldn't very well leave him to suffer," Viola smiled. Digby nodded. He looked very pale. For the first time, Viola saw the *real* Digby. Behind all the bravado and bullying, he was a sensitive soul. They continued walking in silence before Digby stopped.

"I heard about your enquiries into the Brookwater Lane robberies," Digby said, turning to the pair. "If you ask me, you're onto something there."

"Really? You believe us?" Viola asked, shocked that finally someone was on their side. Digby nodded, as he moved the pair to a wall. What he was about to tell them had to be said quietly, he couldn't risk being overheard.

"I believe you because I know who is committing the robberies," Digby whispered.

"George Plumb," Teddy interrupted, too impatient to wait. Digby looked shocked.

"Why, yes. How did you know?"

"We've been doing our own investigation. And we know that you and Plumb are working together," Viola said sternly.

"Yes, but I'm not involved in the robberies!" Digby exclaimed. "I do some work for the gang now and again, offering protection to businesses in return for money."

"Protection, from what?" Viola frowned, remembering the list of shops that she found in Plumb's cabin. Digby took a breath. He spoke quickly and quietly.

"From *who* more like. If a business pays us money, we make sure they are left alone. Make sure they are off limits from..."

"Maltoolers," Viola nodded. Digby shrugged, he'd obviously never spoken to the Emerald Lady before.

"If a business refuses to pay for our protection, the Governor makes sure they regret it. He puts them on his hit list and makes Plumb rob them. It's terrible but I'm not involved with the robbing, I promise you. I don't want anything to do with any of this anymore. Brookwater Lane is like my second home, I'd never do anything to hurt you people." Digby sounded genuinely upset at the situation.

"That must have been what angered Father. I saw a terrifying man argue with him a few days ago. Father told him he wasn't interested," Viola whispered. Teddy gasped.

"Yes, I know. That's why the bakery is on the list. That man you saw would have been Mr Crabtree. He's awful. He's the Governor's muscle and Plumb is his stealer," Digby sighed. "I can't escape. The Governor is vicious and says that once you're in his gang, you never leave."

"Maybe we can help you with that," Teddy sighed. He spoke slowly and firmly. "If you knew who the Governor was, you could expose him and get your freedom back, yes?"

Digby nodded.

"Luckily for you, we do," Teddy smiled.

Digby's eyes widened and he moved a step closer to Teddy, utterly intrigued.

"And?"

"It's Constable Clancy."

Digby fell silent.

"No..."

Teddy nodded.

"That was our response. It's shocking, isn't it?"

"No, I mean, you're wrong. It isn't Clancy."

Teddy rolled his eyes and let out a laugh.

"We should never have trusted you, Digby. This is all just a big joke to you, isn't it? We've helped you and all you can do is -"

"Stop, Teddy!" Digby said, raising his hands. "I do believe you but I promise, it isn't Clancy."

"Well, who is it then?" Viola asked angrily.

"I can't tell you."

"Digby -" Teddy took a step towards him.

"I can't tell you because I don't know. I only ever deal with Plumb and Crabtree but I know it *isn't* Clancy. He's just as determined as you are to see them behind bars. He's not your man, but you mustn't give up. You are close to bringing the Governor down, and I will help you however I can."

# Chapter Eighteen
## *The Great Escape*

Bertha sat in an office at the police station opposite a sergeant who was apparently too busy writing on a piece of paper to pay her any attention. She had asked him three times how long they planned on keeping her there, but he hadn't offered any response. She had spent the night in what the officer referred to as a 'holding cell' and she hadn't slept a wink. It turns out that police stations are very loud places at night-time.

Unfortunately, being arrested was nothing new for Bertha but her crimes were considered so petty, usually tarot reading or "satanic nonsense," as the police referred to it, that they normally let her go after an hour or two. She had nothing to do with the devil, of course, but they never seemed to believe her.

Eventually the office door opened and a policeman entered.

"Someone's here to see you," he sighed. Bertha sensed he was fed up of his job.

"About time," she said, sitting up in her chair. As the policeman made his way further into the office, the solicitor, Mr Collicott followed.

"Good morning, Miss Bard." He put a briefcase on the table and sat down beside the officer opposite her.

"Gus!" she exhaled. "Thank the Lord in heaven that you're here! You've got to get me out."

"Could I have a moment of privacy with Ms Bard, please?" Mr Collicott asked the police officer, who nodded and left the room.

"Miss Bard -"

"Please, call me Bertha. You've known me long enough!" She smiled, beyond happy that he was there to help her. He had helped her once before, when Bertha had fallen off her horse, Consort, and landed in a heap on the ground in the middle of the market. She was convinced she had broken her ankle and cried out for help, but none was forthcoming. That was until Mr Collicott appeared. He helped her to her feet and took her to Dr Anderson who said she hadn't broken anything and just needed to rest. Mr Collicott gave her some money and some food and visited her wagon a few times to make sure she was getting better. That was when she vowed to never ride Consort again. He loved nothing more than to throw people off him and she wasn't prepared to go through that ordeal again, I can tell you.

"I don't believe this is the time for informalities. You shall call me Mr Collicott and I shall call you Miss Bard," he said, opening his case and removing some paperwork. Bertha frowned.

"Fair enough. Seems a bit silly though, don't it? Oh, before I forget, there's a small green box in my wagon with some money in it. I've put it in me birdcage under a sheet. Nobody but me knows it's there. Help yourself to a guinea or two for your trouble. It's all I've got but I realise you need payin'. No one works for free in this life."

Mr Collicott sighed.

"Let's get to the point in hand, shall we? You are accused of some very serious crimes, Miss Bard. Robbery, arson and criminal damage. I doubt you'll be a free woman again in your lifetime," he said bluntly.

"Pardon?" Bertha was shocked at such a claim. "But I didn't do nothing!"

"That's not what the police think." Collicott shuffled papers on the table.

"But you can help me prove 'em wrong! It's that George Plumb. He's a skilamalink and a meater. He's the one behind all these robberies and he has a boss - they call him the Governor." Bertha was firm with her words. Collicott sighed.

"Yes, the police have told me all about your wild stories -"

"They ain't wild!" Bertha wailed. "We have proof!"

Mr Collicott stopped shuffling papers and looked at her.

"Such as?"

"Viola found a button at the watchmakers that we reckon fell off Plumb's coat. Viola noticed that his coat was missing a button, see. It was the exact same button she found at the scene of the crime. And that's just for starters."

Mr Collicott raised an eyebrow, listening to every word.

"Go on."

"We also found a list of shops that Mr Plumb had in his cabin and an address that fell out of his pocket while he was snooping about outside the haberdashery; the Old Lady of Threadneedle Street. That's the Bank of England, by the way."

"Yes, I'm aware of its moniker. Where is the button now?"

"Clancy has it. But we have reason to believe that he ain't to be trusted." Bertha sat forward in her chair and whispered. "We believe he is the Governor."

"Clancy?" Collicott smiled. "That's interesting. And the notes? Did you give them to Constable Clancy too?"

"No. I have 'em 'ere," she said, digging into her pocket. She handed them to Mr Collicott who studied the writing. He took a sharp intake of breath and placed the notes in his case.

"I am afraid that the evidence is very much stacked against you, Miss Bard." He sat back in his chair. "And I feel you have misunderstood why I'm here. I'm here as the solicitor for the prosecution, not the defence."

Bertha laughed bluntly. "Sorry, Gus. For a moment then I thought you said you were here for the prosecution -"

Mr Collicott sniffed and looked up from the table.

"You heard me correctly. I am here to make sure you go to prison for what you have done."

"Excuse me?" Bertha said indignantly. She couldn't believe what he was saying to her. "But I just told you about the button and the notes -"

"Yes, and you should have been more careful, Ms Bard. That's just the sort of thing I could use against you in a court of law."

"I didn't do anything wrong. I saw Plumb robbin' the haberdashery, just as Viola saw 'im robbing the butchers and the watchmakers – she even saw him set the place alight. You have to believe us, Gus. You have to!" she wailed.

"The problem you have is that you are a very dishonest woman, Bard. You lie for a living. Do you honestly think a Judge would believe the word of a charlatan?"

"But the notes and the button –"

"This list is utter nonsense. And you have an address on a scrap of paper? That's simply drivel. You cannot propose in a courtroom that one of the most respectable Constables in this establishment is a crook. You'd be laughed out of London."

"Is there nothing you can do to help me? As my friend?" Bertha cried, tears filling her eyes.

"I can pray for you. May God have mercy on your soul." With that, he stood from the table, closed his case and adjusted his cravat.

"I'm not guilty, Gus! Truly I ain't!" she cried, tears falling. Mr Collicott shook his head in disbelief as he pulled his leather gloves on.

"When you finally realise the best thing is to come clean and confess, send for me," he sighed, placing a small card on the table before leaving the office. "I'll try my best to save you from the gallows."


Viola hadn't heard from Bertha for a few days and she was growing concerned for her friend. Word had spread that the haberdashery had been burgled and she was desperate to talk to her about what

Digby had told them. If Clancy wasn't the Governor, Bertha may have an idea who was. Aside from Adam Clancy, Viola only knew of two people who shared the initials A and C; Annie Cuthbert, an elderly nun, and Arthur Carter, who she believed died two years ago. Neither were a viable suspect, I think you'll agree.

As Viola and Flo reached Bertha's wagon, they stopped and said hello to her two horses, Prince and Consort, who Bertha had named after Queen Victoria's husband, Albert, in his role as the Monarch's husband. As they got closer to the wagon, Viola saw that the door was slightly ajar.

Presuming Bertha was inside, Viola pushed the door open. She froze when she saw that Bertha's once neat and tidy, cosy home was now the scene of chaos. All the beautiful throws and cushions lay strewn across the floor, all her cupboards and drawers were open and the contents spewed all over. The delicate bird cage was smashed on the floor and the candles scattered.

"Oh no," Viola gasped, opening the door for Flo to see. As they made their way inside, shocked and heartbroken at the state of the wagon, the small door at the back of the wagon flew open. Plumb burst out, clutching the Book of Names and a small green box that Viola hadn't seen before.

"You!" Viola gasped, her insides turning to ice.

"Out of my way!" he boomed, pushing past Flo and out of the wagon.

Viola and Flo raced after him but by the time they were out of the vardo, he had made his way towards the dense woodland. They'd never catch him.

Thinking fast, Viola ran to the black horse, Prince. Flo gasped, knowingly. Neither girl had ever been on a horse before and had no idea what to do. Viola, using the steps of the wagon as a way of getting on to his back, pulled herself up and onto the horse.

"Quickly!" Viola cried, pointing to Consort. Flo sighed and climbed, awkwardly, on to the grey horse who puffed his breath out causing his lips to vibrate noisily. Flo wasn't sure if that was a good sign or not.

Viola looked down at Prince and tried to remember what the riders did when she'd seen the horses in the town. Prince didn't have any reigns, so Viola had to grip on to the horse's thick, muscular neck.

"Giddy up!" Viola yelled, having heard a groomer shout that once. She lightly squeezed her ankles into his torso and within seconds, he moved like a thunder bolt. Viola struggled to keep balance, her little body bouncing around with every movement. She glanced back and saw that Flo was following – but she too was struggling with the velocity of the speeding horse.  The girls screamed as the horses picked up pace, but they were catching up with Plumb. As the horses found their rhythm, the girls seemed to find theirs – they were gripping with all their might and somehow, they were staying on. The horses flew through the woodland, dodging trees and fallen trunks, obviously loving the freedom of an inexperienced rider.

Plumb, too, was running through the woodland but, being a measly human, he couldn't outrun two speeding horses. Viola could see he was starting to slow and was getting out of breath.  With every step, they were gaining on him and before long they were just a few feet away but he wouldn't give up. He kept checking behind him as the horses closed in.

"You've got nowhere to run, Plumb!" Viola yelled as the horse was within touching distance of him. Suddenly, he darted to the right and looked back at them with a smile.

Viola's horse saw the lake first.

Being afraid of the water, Prince pulled back, almost throwing Viola off. She screamed and desperately grabbed the horse's mane as the only way of keeping on. Flo's horse, however, hadn't seen the water until it was too late. He bucked, throwing Flo off his back. Flo screamed as her tiny body shot up into the air, terrified for her life.

Viola watched with hopeless fear as Flo plummeted into the water with an almighty splash.

"Noooooooo!" Viola screamed, clambering off her horse to get to her friend. Flo thrashed around in the water, desperate for air.

"I…can't…swim!" she cried, flapping and splashing in the water. Viola gasped, fearful for her friend. She pulled off her coat and threw it towards Flo, keeping hold of one arm.

"Take my coat – I'll pull you in!" she cried, getting as close to the end of the mud as she could. Flo reached for the coat but couldn't get a grip.

"I…can't…" Flo spluttered, swallowing mouthfuls of murky water.

"Try again – you can do it," Viola cried. Flo reached out again but this time she grabbed the other arm of the coat. Viola pulled her to the edge of the lake and up onto dry land. Gasping and clutching for air, Flo lay on the grassy river bank. Her beautiful apple-green dress was now a horrid shade of mud. Viola rubbed her back and told her she was safe now.

"Better luck next time!" Plumb laughed, having watched the events unfold from a distance. Viola turned and glared at the rogue.

"This isn't over," she hissed. He laughed even louder and turned, disappearing into the woodland. Viola knew that Flo was in no state to continue the chase so she sat with her until she felt strong enough to get up.

They decided it was best to walk back with Prince and Consort rather than try to ride them again. Flo's back was aching terribly and her favourite dress was soaking wet, but thankfully, she was spared any serious injury. It took them a little while to reach the wagon but as they approached, they saw Constable Clancy sitting on the step. He stood when he saw them.

"I have some news," he said solemnly. "Bertha's been arrested for the robberies in Brookwater Lane."

Bertha sat staring into space. She had only managed an hour's sleep last night in the cold, stony cell. She couldn't stop replaying the conversation she had had with Collicott that day. Why wasn't he willing to help her? Why was he so convinced that she was guilty? She didn't want to keep thinking about it but she couldn't switch her brain off. She was exhausted and in need of something hot to drink. Even her bones felt cold. The police had offered her a piece of dry bread and some water, but that was a few hours ago now and she would kill for a cuppa. Not literally, of course. She was in enough trouble as it was.

She had asked a passing policeman if she could have a cup of tea but judging by his snort of a response that wasn't going to happen. She sat back on the bench, peering through the bars at two officers deep in conversation. They were too far away for Bertha to be able hear what they were saying but she could sense it was a discussion about what to do with her. Her brain was working double quick – she had to think of a way to get out of this place.

Suddenly, desperate cries rang out from within the cell next to her. All the police officers raced into the holding cell and gathered round a lad who was lying on the floor, coughing and spluttering.

"He's choking! Get a doctor!" cried a fellow prisoner. Bertha stood in horror. She could see Stanley Smith, or the Purple Pickpocket as Viola had named him, lying on the floor with police officers grouped around him. He was facing Bertha, but he was thrashing around, fighting for his life. Bertha watched in shock at the poor lad, willing him to be alright. As she looked at him, he wriggled on the floor, desperately clambering at the officer that was helping him. He reached into the policeman's pocket and pulled out a set of keys. At bullet speed, he had put them on the floor and pushed them over to Bertha. He opened his eyes, just for a second, and stared right her. He glanced over to the door before continuing his fake choking. Bertha knew this was her chance to escape, she grabbed the keys, quietly opened the cell and walked out, dropping the keys to the floor.

Bertha climbed the ladder to the treehouse, puffing and wheezing as she did so. She had run all the way from the station to the treehouse and was now feeling very light headed and dizzy. She had pulled her shawl up and over her head to try and disguise herself. She was a fugitive now, after all.

"Bertha!" Viola cried as she poked her head through the floor of the treehouse.

"You managed to get out!" Flo beamed.

"Just about," Bertha puffed. "It was the strangest thing. Stanley Smith, the pickpocket, well, he just collapsed and started pretending to choke. Obviously, the police rushed to his aid and the cheeky thing stole their keys so that I could make my escape. Most peculiar."

Viola smiled.

"I knew he was in and out of those cells like a Jack in the Box so I asked if he could somehow help to get you out. He was a little reluctant at first, but then I told him about all the naughtiness I see him get up to. He was suddenly very willing to help."

"You did that?" Bertha was shocked.

"Of course! We had to get you out of there," Viola shrugged. "It was a lot easier than I thought, actually. He's quite a nice lad."

Bertha smiled and pulled Viola in for a hug. It was a wonderful feeling having someone on her side for once. She eventually let Viola go and sat up, wiping her tears on her gloves. Flo beamed and handed her a steaming hot mug of tea. Bertha cheered as she scooped it up and held it to her cheek. The warmth was incredible.

"Thank you, my angels," she smiled. "I'm sorry girls, but I'm afraid I 'ave more bad news," Bertha sighed, staring at the drink. Viola touched her hand.

"We already know," she said softly. "The robbery at your wagon?"

"You what?" Bertha asked, shocked by this revelation.

"It was in a bad state, I can tell you. I'm afraid he stole your Book of Names," Viola shook her head, replaying the image of the destroyed wagon.

"And a green box," Flo added.

Bertha froze.

Suddenly the mug she was holding crashed to the floor spilling the hot tea everywhere. Bertha's hands shook with fear.

"Oh, good heavens," she whispered. "That box contains me life savings. I'm finished."

"Bertha..." Viola started.

"And if that book gets in the wrong hands..."

"We saw who robbed you, Bertha. It was Plumb," Viola said. Bertha nodded.

"I knew it. When did this happen, girls?"

This morning," Viola said. "We were on our way to tell you about the robbery at the haberdashery when we saw him. We gave chase but...we couldn't keep up with him." She decided to omit the part where Bertha's horse threw Flo into a lake. Bertha was already feeling bad, she didn't need to make the situation worse.

"Clancy was waiting for us when we got back to the wagon and he told us about your arrest." Flo added.

"How convenient," Bertha hissed. "I told Gus about that money box last night when I thought he would need payin' to help me. He must have told Clancy about it and he sent in Plumb."

Viola frowned. Bertha rolled her eyes and told them about Mr Collicott working for the prosecution and how betrayed she felt by her so-called friend.

"I'm done for, girls. Gus is the best solicitor in the whole of London and he's working for the enemy," Bertha said tearfully.

"I'm sorry," Viola said genuinely. "We will clear your name, I promise."

Flo looked over at Bertha's open bag and frowned. "What's that?" she said, pointing to the business card.

"Oh, that's for when I change me mind and come clean. Which I won't, of course because I ain't done nothing wrong. I can't believe me bad luck, girls. I thought Gus was me friend. He's probably sittin' in his fancy office in Pennyworth Mews, right now. Not a care in the world, and here I am, a fugitive," Bertha closed her eyes and rested her head against the wall of the treehouse. Her body was so exhausted that she almost fell asleep there and then.

Viola started to do up her coat and tighten her scarf.

"What are you doing?" Flo whispered.

"I'm going to pay Mr Collicott a visit. I'll prove to him that Bertha is innocent," Viola said quietly.

# Chapter Nineteen
### *Pennyworth Mews*

Viola had been watching the offices of Collicott Law for a while now. It was situated in a very grand looking building with a huge black front door in the middle of Pennyworth Mews. The windows had very expensive looking curtains hanging inside them, and Viola wondered just how exquisite it was inside. She'd find out soon enough.

So far, her observations had only seen one man go into the building and that was quite some time ago. She was beginning to doubt whether her plan would work when the same man eventually reappeared. As the door closed behind him, he put his top hat back on and straightened his coat. He walked down the many steps to the street and checked his pocket watch before setting off. Viola raced to be in front of him, setting her plan into action.

Ensuring she was now in the man's eye line, she deliberately fell to the floor, letting out a cry of pain. Naturally, the man rushed to her aid.

"My dear, are you hurt? That was quite a tumble!" the man said, helping her to her feet.

"I...I don't f-fink so, fank you sir. I'm just so clumsy, sir. Me muffher will not be pleased if I tore me new dress." She was mimicking the voices of Bertha and Plumb and felt quite pleased with her impression so far. The man let out a sympathetic sound and reached into his pocket.

"You poor thing. Here, I'm sure this will more than make up for it," he handed her a few gold coins. Viola gulped. She wasn't expecting any money.

"Fank you, sir!" she beamed. "What's ya name? I'd like to tell me muffher who 'elped me today."

"Dickens. Charles Dickens," he smiled, tipping his hat. He smiled at Viola and walked away. Viola put the coins in her pocket, dusted herself down and skipped up the steps.

The office of Collicott Law was indeed, very grand. The walls were covered in fine art including a huge portrait of Queen Victoria. It was exceptionally painted but scared Viola a little. Her eyes seemed to follow Viola around the room.

There was a rather stern looking old woman sitting behind a small oak desk with several tall leather wing-backed chairs opposite her. A record player, or perhaps it was a gramophone, sat in the corner softly playing music whilst an open fire crackled.

"Can I help you?" the stern woman asked, looking as if an

unpleasant smell had appeared under her nose.

"I am here to see Mr Collicott, please. I have some very urgent information about his client, Mr Dickens," she replied confidently. The woman raised an eyebrow and glared at Viola for a second, assessing whether she was telling the truth. Viola glared back, not budging. The woman sighed and stood up, going to an office door behind her. She opened it and peered round.

"Sir..."

"Miss Etheridge!" boomed the voice of Mr Collicott from behind the door, "I have told you repeatedly to knock before you enter my office. Good grief, woman."

"I do apologise, Mr Collicott, sir." Miss Etheridge snipped. "There is a young girl here, sir. She says she has some urgent information about Mr Dickens - sir."

"Really? How peculiar. Well, don't just stand there, woman, show her in," he snarled. Viola took a breath and followed Miss Etheridge into his office.

"You!" he said, standing from his chair.

"Thank you, Miss Etheridge, that will be all," Viola said, using an expression she had heard customers say to their carriage drivers many times. Miss Etheridge's jaw dropped as Mr Collicott chuckled. The door slammed shut as she left the room.

"What information do you have on my client?" he asked, sitting back down. Viola chose to remain standing.

"Nothing. I lied," Viola said firmly. "I didn't think you'd see me if I told you it was to do with Bertha Bard."

Collicott pursed his lips.

"That frightful woman is missing from police custody. Do you know of her whereabouts?"

"Bertha's innocent. You need to help me clear her name and put the real criminal behind bars. George Plumb is the guilty man and he's working for someone called the Gov-"

"Please, stop. I have heard this countless times. Bertha, Clancy - even Miss Etheridge has told me this story. And that is exactly what this is. A *story*."

"You may have already heard it, but you haven't heard it from me."

Collicott took a big intake of breath.

"You are friends with this gypsy woman, aren't you? The woman who lies to people every day of her life? The woman who claims that she speaks to the dead? The woman who would steal from her own grandmother if the price was right?" He sat back in his chair. Viola frowned.

"She's not a liar. She *can* speak to the dead."

"Has she ever spoken to someone you know in the heavens?" he asked. Viola went to answer, but couldn't.

"My point exactly. I'm sorry, Miss Pumpernickel, truly I am. I believe you have been tricked by a very clever con woman. Perhaps you ought to go home and forget all about her."

Viola sighed. She didn't want to believe Collicott but he gave a compelling case. She could see why he was such a successful solicitor.

"You're not going to help her, are you?" Viola whispered.

Collicott looked up at her.

"No, I'm not. I'm sorry."

Viola looked to the floor and began to cry. Tears streamed uncontrollably from her eyes. Her sobbing made Collicott increasingly uncomfortable and he stood to go to her.

"I'm sorry, sir. I didn't want to cry," she wailed. He nervously patted her twice on the shoulder and then stood back.

"There, there," he said, unsure of what to do. He didn't like it when people cried, especially girls. "You'll get over this soon enough."

Viola nodded.

"Do you have a handkerchief, please?" Viola sniffed. He rolled his eyes and went to his briefcase as Viola moved closer to his desk. He opened his case and pulled out his hanky. Handing it to her, he opened the office door. Sensing that she had outstayed her welcome, she wiped her eyes and handed it back, said goodbye and left the office. As she raced down the steps onto the street, the sad frown quickly turned into a big grin.

"Penny for a lady?" an old woman said, sitting at the foot of the steps. She was dressed in shabby clothes and looked very cold and rather poorly. Several people passed her by, ignoring her pleas. Viola walked up to her and handed her the coins that Mr Dickens gave her.

"Bless you, child," the woman said, her face lighting up with happiness.

Viola smiled back and raced to the treehouse, desperate to tell the others about the letter she had just secretly taken from his desk whilst his back was turned.

## Chapter Twenty
*Secrets and Lies*

Viola stood in shock, looking at Bertha's face on the poster in front of her. In fact, this was just one of nearly twenty that were plastered all over the city.

"WANTED for robbery and arson. To any person who shall give information leading to the arrest of Miss Bertha Bard, Her Majesty's Government hereby offer a reward of £50, payable on conviction."

Viola had read the words over and over and they still didn't seem real. She was on her way from Collicott's office to the treehouse when she saw them. Teddy appeared at her shoulder and tutted as he read the words splashed across the paper.

"We'll clear her name, don't worry, girl," Teddy said. Viola nodded but said nothing. "Where have you been?"

"I went to see Mr Collicott to try and convince him of Bertha's innocence. I feel that he knows more than he is letting on, I just don't know what," she said, not expecting him to be able to answer, of course.

"You did what?" Teddy asked, shocked. "You could have got yourself in real trouble, Viola."

"I know, I know. But I didn't tell him where Bertha is. I'm not silly."

Teddy rolled his eyes and suggested they get out of Brookwater Lane as soon as they could, police were everywhere and he didn't want to risk being overheard.

They could hear Bertha's snores from twenty feet away. At first, Viola thought a wild animal had climbed into the treehouse, but as they got closer, she realised it was Bertha's nose making the dreadful sound.

As Viola climbed the ladder and crawled into the house, Walpole trotted over to her and let out a friendly meow. Viola tickled his chin and gently nudged Bertha awake as Teddy made his way up to the house.

"Not the chicken!" she cried as she sat upright. Viola giggled at the sight of a sleepy Bertha who hadn't quite woken up yet. She snorted and rubbed her eyes before realising where she was. "Viola? Teddy? When did you get here?" she asked.

"A moment ago," Teddy smiled.

"Any news?" Bertha yawned. Viola took a moment before answering.

"I went to visit Mr Collicott at his office today. Please, don't tell me off," she said, lifting a hand as Bertha went to speak. "I asked him for his help. I explained that you were innocent but he wasn't interested."

"I told you. Sorry you wasted your time."

"Oh, it was far from a waste of time, Bertha. I got the feeling that he was somehow protecting Plumb. So, I pretended to get upset and as he went to fetch a handkerchief, I grabbed this," she said, pulling a letter out of her apron pocket. She handed it to Bertha who looked at it, confused.

"I don't understand," she said with a frown. "It's just a letter to a client. What does this have to do with me?"

"His S's are backwards, just like on the notes we have found," Viola smiled. "I think Gus Collicott wrote them. We just need to work out why."

Every year in Brookwater Lane, the Wintertide Festival took place. There had been talk of cancelling the event due to the unfortunate robberies and fires, but the residents had decided to continue nonetheless. Mr Pumpernickel had said that they must put on a united front against the criminals and show that they weren't afraid of them.

Clancy had been to the shop every day asking Viola if she knew where Bertha was hiding. And every day Viola would have to lie and say she didn't. She hated being dishonest, especially to someone she once held in such high regard, but she couldn't risk

Bertha ending up in jail. Thankfully, only the Pumpernickels and Flo knew about the treehouse so she was safe for a while, at least.

As usual, all the market workers and shopkeepers would decorate their stalls and windows in a wintery fashion to make it all look lovely and festive. This year was no different. With Christmas wreaths and holly, pine cones and beautiful flowers, Brookwater Lane looked truly magnificent. Winter was always Viola's favourite time of year. She didn't like being cold, however, but she knew that the snowy days would lead up to Christmas and that was always wonderful.

The buzz on Brookwater Lane was that the Mayor of London, Sir William Farncombe, had agreed to come along and meet the residents of Brookwater Lane. Perhaps he felt he wanted to pass on his condolences regarding the recent terrible events.

A large crowd had gathered in front of a wooden stage created for the Mayor to speak to his public and for various presentations to take place. Mrs Pumpernickel was hoping to win 'Best Floral Design' for the fifth year in a row for her outstanding work in decorating the wreaths. She had become a bit of a celebrity for her breath-taking designs and always donated her winnings to the orphanage.

"Ladies and gentlemen!" boomed the loud voice of Mr Wiggins, the manager of the Wilton's Theatre. Viola recognised him as the man handing out flyers for Ruby Dancer. His voice was incredibly rich and powerful and Viola realised why he worked in the theatre. "We are very excited to be holding the tenth annual Wintertide Festival. I must say that all the shops and stalls look truly amazing. You must all be very proud of your efforts. So, without further ado, please join me in welcoming to the stage, our faithful mayor, Sir William Farncombe!" he said, followed by rapturous applause from the audience.

The Mayor of London slowly made his way to the centre of the stage, waving and smiling to the crowd, enjoying the attention. He was dressed in the finest clothes Viola had ever seen. His dark navy trousers were tucked into some long silk socks that looked brand new. He wore a heavy red and white fur cape over a crisp, white shirt that fitted him perfectly. He really was very fancy indeed.

"Thank you, thank you. You are too kind." His voice was as aristocratic as you were ever likely to hear. "First and foremost, I must commend the residents of Brookwater Lane on their resilience and strength in what must be very trying and worrying times. You have shown that you, the working-class people of London, will not be terrified and overpowered by the criminal underworld. I just hope, for your sake, that these dreadful villains have given up their campaign of terror," he said, again followed by an eruption of cheers and claps. As he said the final line, Mr Collicott entered the stage and stood next to Sir William, who acknowledged him with a smile.

"I must also thank today's benefactor, Mr Collicott of Collicott Law. A fine man, I think you will agree." Sir William announced to the crowd. For a third time, the crowd went wild with applause.

"Thank you, Sir Bill," Collicott laughed. "As some of you know, I have been working as a solicitor now for almost twenty years, and I have nothing but respect and love for the people of

Brookwater Lane. I hope that the collection raised will go some way towards helping to rebuild their livelihoods. Please rest assured that the criminal behind these terrible crimes is in our sights; a criminal with a brash nature and unyielding belief that she is innocent which will make her imprisonment even sweeter."

Viola knew he was talking about Bertha. One word from him and the whole of London could turn against her. Especially with Sir William Farncombe on his side.

"Bertha Bard is a common criminal. She is a thief, a liar and a charlatan. She claims to be able to speak to the dead – an utterly absurd claim, I think you will agree. She preys on the weak and the vulnerable and tricks them out of their hard-earned money. She is, however, on the run, having escaped police custody. But rest assured, we will find her."

Viola's blood was boiling. She'd heard enough of these dreadful fabrications. Sensing that his sister was about to explode with rage, Teddy took her arm and held her back.

"I have in my hand a book that belongs to Miss Bard." Mr Collicott held the leather book above his head for all to see. Viola gasped as she looked at Teddy, who understood exactly what she was thinking.

*Plumb stole that book from the wagon - how did Collicott get hold of it?*

"This book contains information that will both shock and appal," Collicott continued. "There is a substantial reward for Bertha's capture, and I beg anyone who is housing this fugitive to hand her over."

The crowd started whispering amongst themselves, which worried Viola.

*What if someone had seen her in the treehouse?*

Her heart was thumping.

"Bertha refers to this as her Book of Names. She learns of a recent passing and hounds the authorities for information on the deceased. I will read a few lines, if you'll indulge me for one moment?" he asked the crowd who cheered their agreement. Viola stood, frozen to the spot as he read. "George Jones, 50, died of small pox. No money, no family. Cecila Dean, 28, died of tuberculous, poor parents and no money. Michael Murray, 62, died of alcohol, wife and children. Wealthy. Lives near Kensington Palace...more investigation needed."

Viola looked up at Teddy.

"I don't understand what he is doing," she whispered.

Teddy closed his eyes.

"Bertha's made a list of everyone who died and whether they were rich or not," he said, sadly. Viola's mind was racing.

*Why would she make such a list?*

"John Bramble," Collicott spoke slowly and deliberately. "Aged 57, died of consumption, wife Emily and daughter, Florence. No money but brother-in-law is a Judge. Vast wealth."

Viola felt sick as the realisation that he was talking about Flo's father washed over her.

"Come on, let's go home," Teddy said, trying to take Viola away from this horrible situation. As he turned them away from the stage, they saw Flo standing in the crowd, frozen to the spot. Tears were spilling out of her eyes as she stared at Viola.

"Is this true?" Flo whimpered, her voice cracking with emotion. "Was Bertha only friends with me to get to my uncle's money?"

"I don't know, Flo. But if she was, I will never speak to her again."

Bertha was completely unprepared for the onslaught heading her way. From Brookwater Lane to the treehouse in Hyde Park, Viola had been stewing on what Collicott has said. By the time she had reached Bertha, she was overflowing with rage; a rage that nobody had ever experienced before.

"Is it true?" Viola screamed. Bertha jumped at the sheer volume of her words.

"Is what true, darling?" she replied.

"Do not call me darling!" Viola yelled. "Mr Collicott read out passages from your Book of Names to the whole of Brookwater Lane. He told everyone how you made a record of people who have died and you made a note of how much money they were worth."

"Yes," Bertha said, nodding.

"You don't deny it?" Teddy asked, surprised.

"No, of course I don't. I don't understand why you are so angry. You know what I am. That I speak to the dead."

"I believed you, Bertha. I trusted you. Even when Constable Clancy told me not to, even when my own mother told me not to - but they were right, weren't they? You trick people into thinking you are talking to the dead but you're lying. You simply scour the local newspaper for reports of people's deaths and keep some morbid account of their wealth and then con the family out of their money. And Flo's family? How dare you!" Viola was utterly livid.

"Let me explain…" Bertha started but Viola couldn't hear her for rage.

"Leave me alone. I never want to speak to you again," Viola hissed. She turned and climbed down the rope ladder as quickly as she could. Bertha tried calling after her but Viola ignored her cries.

"Teddy?" Bertha said, her voice weak.

"You heard her. Leave us alone," he said quietly, following his sister down the tree to the park.

# Chapter Twenty-One
### *A Welcome Distraction*

Viola felt numb inside.

She didn't fancy talking to anyone and so kept herself to herself for a while. Her parents were naturally concerned about their chatterbox daughter being so quiet but hoped that it would pass in time. They had tried to distract her with books or tasks in the shop but nothing would interest her for long. She missed Bertha and Walpole terribly and felt deeply hurt by the betrayal. How could she trust anyone again?

One afternoon, as she stood in Brookwater Lane, avoiding the Man with the Silver Cane as he walked past the bakery, Walpole appeared at her feet. She gasped and bent down to stroke his warm fur. As she did so, she noticed he had a note attached to his collar. It was from Bertha:

*Dearest Viola,*

*Please speak to me. I ain't the liar you think I am.*

*You must believe me.*

*Walpole and I miss you and Flo greatly.*

*Love Bertha – The Emerald Lady.*

Viola screwed up the note and threw it into a passing dust cart.

The next day, she sat in the treehouse, holding her grandfather's pocket watch, wishing he was there to make her laugh with a silly story about pirates or wizards, but thinking of him only made her feel worse. As she put the watch back in her apron, she spotted a golden bell lying on the treehouse floor in the corner. She picked it up and studied it.

It was from Bertha's shawl. She remembered how, at first, she was terrified of the *jangle jangle* of the bells and the mysterious Emerald Lady. Then later, of course, how happy she was when she heard it in the distance because that meant Bertha and Walpole were on their way and an adventure was sure to be had.

She sighed and flicked the bell down onto the grass.

*Time to move on*, Viola told herself before climbing down the ladder.

Mary Pumpernickel couldn't remember the last time she sat down.

She had been exceptionally busy from the moment she woke up. Her day had consisted of a trip to the market to get some fruit and vegetables, making several soups with said produce, helped at the hospital as a voluntary nurse and then she called in to the orphanage on Petticoat Road to drop off some of the soup. She was now heading home to prepare the dinner and put the children to bed for the evening, having picked up some flour on her way. She had agreed to bake a cake for Dr Anderson's wife's birthday, a decision she was now regretting.

Her feet were aching and her back was tired but she never complained. She had to keep the house running or it would simply fall apart; the children would go hungry and the bakery would grind to a halt.

She finally reached the bakery and made her way up the steps to her home, saying hello to a few of the market traders as she passed. She pushed open the door, desperate to put down the heavy load. She almost fell into the room as the door opened and she finally put the flour on the ground. She stretched as she stood, rubbing her lower back. She took off her coat and called out a hello to her family.

"Good evening, dear," chirped the voice of her husband from the living room. She pushed open the door and stopped in her tracks.

"What on earth?" Her jaw dropped. Mr Pumpernickel was sitting in his regular armchair, reading a newspaper. That wasn't the shocking part, of course, he did that every evening. No, the shock was Viola sitting on the floor surrounded by piles of discarded clothes, sewing a pair of Teddy's trousers.

"Hello, Mother," she beamed, looking up at her.

"Viola Ivy Pumpernickel! What are you doing?" Mary gasped, utterly confused.

"I'm learning to sew. I have unpicked all the trousers, dresses and skirts that I could find. I'm teaching myself to put them all back together again."

"She's really rather good," Mr Pumpernickel smiled proudly, peering over his paper.

"*A-all* of the trousers? *A-all* of my dresses?" Mary stuttered. Viola nodded.

"Every single one of them," she smiled. Mary put her hand to her chest and took a moment.

"I'll make some tea," she said quietly. "And then I'll help you sew them all back together."

"No need. I'm almost finished. Father's trousers were a little tricky because I think you had already repaired them a few times, but I'm sure I've done it," she said, concentrating on the needle and thread in her hand. "You were right, Mama. This really is rather fun!"

Mary slowly made her way over to the pile of clothes and picked up one of Viola's aprons. She studied the needlework and nodded.

"My word, you've mastered the slip stitch. Who taught you this?"

"Nobody. I looked at the stiches that were already there before I took them apart and copied them," she said matter-of-factly. She looked up to see her mother admiring some red ribbon she had sewn on the apron. "I thought I would add a bit of colour to make it prettier."

Mary laughed as she put the apron down on the pile. She looked at her husband who was equally impressed.

"It's kept her quiet for hours!" he smiled. Mary reached out And took his hand, giving it a light squeeze. "I think she needed something to distract her from the gypsy woman," he whispered.

"Well done, my darling," she chuckled, looking at her beautiful daughter. "I'm so very proud of you."


Viola had agreed to help Mr Pumpernickel in the bakery the following day. She hadn't done that in a while and missed spending time with her father. She had even volunteered to sweep the shop floor. Mr Pumpernickel had been telling her various stories to try and keep her distracted from Bertha, and Viola was grateful for it. Every now and again she would stop and give her father a cuddle, just to show how grateful she was to have him there.

As Albert was showing Viola how to make the perfect mince pie, the door opened.

"Good morning," Mr Pumpernickel said, looking up at the customer for the first time. "Ah, Mr Collicott."

Viola froze. She looked up at him but said nothing. He was the last person she wanted to see right now.

"Good morning, Albert. Viola," he smiled, removing his hat. "I'd like some of your sultana and banana bread please."

Albert nodded and disappeared out to the back room where they kept extra stock. Viola sighed and looked away. She had nothing to say to him.

"How are you feeling, Miss Pumpernickel? I heard that you had disowned Miss Bard. I think you've made a wise choice."

"I'm fine," Viola hissed. He may have exposed Bertha as a liar and a trickster, but he didn't have to do it in such a cruel manner. Mr Collicott raised an eyebrow and sucked his teeth.

"Viola! I have some news -" Flo cried, rushing into the shop behind Mr Collicott. She stopped when she saw him. "Oh h-hello Mr Collicott."

"Florence Bramble," he pouted. "I was dreadfully sorry to discover that your family had been a target of Miss Bard's. You are a very brave little girl," he said, patting her on the shoulder. Flo shrugged, not sure what to say to him. Thankfully, Mr Pumpernickel came back and handed Mr Collicott his requested loaf. In return, he handed Albert a few coins and offered his thanks. He bid his goodbyes and left the shop.

"Would you like a mince pie, Flo?" Albert said, offering the tray of freshly cooked pies to her. She smiled and reached for the biggest one. Mr Pumpernickel took the tray out to the back and asked the girls to keep an eye on the shop. Once they were alone, Flo rushed to Viola.

"I have some news. I've spoken to my Aunt Eliza. I told her everything about Bertha and the Book of Names. She confirmed that she had done a reading for them, but it seems that Bertha was telling the truth," Flo said. Viola looked at her friend, unsure of how to react.

Flo explained that her auntie and uncle had gone to see Bertha shortly after Mr Bramble died, when Mrs Bramble had just been admitted to hospital. They were desperate to know if Mr Bramble was safe in the heavens and asked that he help poor Emily recover from her dreadful illness. Uncle James had told Bertha that he would continue to go to her for readings until they were able to contact John – he even told her that money was not a problem. Bertha only ever had one reading with them, however, despite this potentially lucrative offer. Bertha had connected with John Bramble in the heavens almost immediately and confirmed he was at peace. He also referred to his wife as "Lola," a nickname that nobody apart from his closest family knew he used. This, Flo said, was enough to confirm to James and Eliza that they were speaking to the real spirit of John Bramble. In other words, Mr Collicott had got it wrong – Bertha hadn't tried to fleece the Brambles out of money at all. In fact, the Book of Names was not a note of recent deaths that she could take advantage of, it was simply a record of the readings Bertha had given.

Viola took a step to process the information.

"Bertha wasn't lying to us?" Viola whispered. Flo shook her head.

"No. We were wrong to listen to Mr Collicott, but why would he lie?" Flo said, utterly confused.

Before Viola could answer, Mr Pumpernickel had returned to the shop. He stopped at the counter and tutted.

"Oh look, Augustus has left his hat behind. Never mind, I'll send Teddy down to his office later," he picked up the hat and placed it on the table at the back. Viola nodded, not really paying much attention. Suddenly, she turned to her father.

"Augustus?" she frowned. "But Mr Collicott's name is Gus."

"Gus is short for Augustus, like we call Edward 'Teddy' or Rupert 'Rupe.' It's just a nickname," he shrugged.

Viola looked at Flo and gasped.

They'd finally found the Governor.

# Chapter Twenty-Two
## *An Underground London*

Viola and Flo rushed to the treehouse, desperate to speak to Bertha and apologise. They also wanted to tell her that they'd worked out who the Governor was once and for all. As they scrambled up the rope, Viola had already started apologising. She poked her head through the hole and stopped. The treehouse was empty of Bertha's blankets and Walpole's bedding. There was no sign that the Emerald Lady and her cat had ever been there.

Realising that Bertha probably felt incredibly alone and unwanted, Viola and Flo decided to try her wagon to see if she had made her way home. Again, there was no sign of her. The destruction caused to the wagon by Plumb's ransacking had been tidied away so it was clear she had been there recently, but she had since disappeared.

Viola and Flo sat on the wagon's steps, wondering where on earth Bertha could be. They felt terrible, imagining how lonely she would be feeling.

"Maybe she's run away," Flo said. "I wouldn't blame her. She thinks we all hate her and the police are after her. She has nowhere left to turn."

Viola shook her head.

"Prince and Consort are both here. She'd never leave them. Plus, look over there," she said, pointing to a fresh pile of hay. "She's been here to feed and water them. And they're wearing fresh rugs. No, she's here somewhere - we just have to think where," Viola said firmly. As they sat in silence, Viola noticed something sparkling in the grass. She walked over and picked up a small golden bell. Then she saw another one a few feet ahead of her, and another one and another one. They seemed to be leading to a large cluster of trees.

"These are from Bertha's shawl," Viola said, showing the handful of bells to Flo. "She must have left them here for us to follow."

"Look, there's another one," Flo said, rushing to the trees. As she crouched down to pick it up, she noticed a piece of wood jutting out from under a large hedgerow. She pushed it back to reveal a small, wooden door in the ground, no bigger than a carriage wheel. She gasped as she turned to Flo.

"I wonder where it leads," Viola said quietly.

"There's only one way to find out," Flo gulped, reaching down and pulling the door open with a creak.

The girls climbed down through the door and found themselves in a dark and cold tunnel several feet underground. It wasn't the sort of place you would want to hide in, given the choice. The stone ground was uneven and slippery due to the residual water that had obviously found its way through from the River Thames. As they walked further within, countless arches lined the tunnel, no doubt leading off to other secret locations throughout London.

*Drip, drip, drip...*

"I'm scared," Flo whispered, gripping Viola's hand tightly; she didn't like the dark at the best of times, let alone when she was trapped under the ground.

"So am I, Flo, but we have to find Bertha. We can't leave her here."

Flo sighed as they continued to walk further into the mysterious tunnel. The air was getting colder and colder, causing them both to shiver.

"I hope it's not haunted," Flo gulped. "I don't fancy meeting a ghost today of all days."

"Of course it's not haunted!" Viola giggled.

"That's what you said about the iron foundry, Viola, but we heard footsteps one night, didn't we? The ghost of Eli Silversmith, Teddy said."

Viola frowned. Perhaps she was right. The foundry was a very creepy place to be at night but at least you could run out of it quick enough. Right now, they were a good ten feet underground which felt very unusual and rather frightening.

"What if someone died trying to get out of here and he just lay undiscovered for years and years?" Viola whispered, letting her imagination run wild again. "His ghost could roam this tunnel for eternity."

"You really are rather dramatic, Viola."

"It could be true," Viola giggled.

All of a sudden, Flo stopped and pointed into the dark shadows.

"There," she whispered. Viola followed her hand to see a bundle of clothes up against the wall of the tunnel. She knew instantly it was Bertha.

Running as fast as she could on the wet stone floor, Viola reached the bundle of clothes and crouched down.

"Bertha?" she whispered. The bundle started to move and a sprout of orange hair poked out from under a blanket. Bertha's face appeared seconds later.

"Viola?" she croaked. Viola's eyes filled with tears and she hugged Bertha tightly.

"You're safe!" Flo smiled.

"Thank heavens you're here," Bertha sniffed. "I thought I'd never see you two again."

Flo bent down and stroked Walpole who had been soundly sleeping next to her. He looked like he needed some food.

"I'm so sorry I didn't believe you, Bertha," Viola whispered. Bertha shook her head and held out her hand.

"My aunt told me about your reading with my family. We know you were telling the truth, don't we?" Flo said, turning to Viola. She bit her lip and took a second before speaking.

"I cannot defend you if I don't know for certain," Viola said carefully. "Prove to me that you can speak to the dead, once and for all."

Bertha nodded and shifted herself to get comfortable.

"Who do you wish me to contact?" Bertha said, looking at Viola.

"My grandfather," Viola replied instantly. Bertha nodded and asked if she had anything on her that belonged to him. Viola took a breath and pulled out the watch. Bertha wrapped her hands around the timepiece and closed her eyes. The girls sat in silence, watching as Bertha remained still – almost in prayer, before she opened her eyes.

"Your grandfather, Edmund. He was a good man. He was trustworthy and honourable and decent. They are few and far between round 'ere. He loved you all so much. You must know that."

Viola nodded with a smile.

Bertha continued. "He was a fisherman and worked hard for his family. He also used to write poems and come up with mystical stories – that's where you get your imagination from, Viola," she smiled.

"Yes, my mother tells me that I remind her of him sometimes."

Bertha nodded.

"He used to tell you stories about magical wizards and wicked witches." Her voice become quiet and serious. "He's telling me that you must believe in magic again. After all, you have magic in your bones. You have the power to change the world."

Viola gasped.

"He used to tell me that all the time! Nobody knows about that, not even Mama."

Bertha paused.

"Oh, good heavens," she said gravely. "Your grandfather, he saw a woman in the water. She couldn't swim, she was drowning. Edmund knew he had to rescue her and so he jumped in without hesitation. That's what he was like, wasn't it? Always thinking of others. He dragged the poor woman to shore but the water was so cold. He fought for his life, Viola. He desperately wanted to survive but the pneumonia was too far gone. Oh, I'm ever so sorry, Viola," Bertha gulped, her voice cracked as tears fell down her cheeks.

"Don't apologise. He saved her. He died a hero," Viola smiled gently.

"He loves you all so much. He says that he knows you are missing him dreadfully but you can still talk to him, sweetheart. He's always listening to you and he's forever in your heart, little cabbage."

Viola beamed as she wiped a tear on her sleeve.

"That was his name for me. It always made me giggle."

Flo put her arm around her, knowing just how much Viola needed this.

"I believe you now, Bertha. I'll defend you till the end," Viola said firmly.

Viola and Flo had managed to get Bertha to Doc's clinic without being seen. They had decided it was the safest place for her to hide for a while. The tunnel was too cold and damp and she was in need of warmth and food. Doc had agreed to look after both Bertha and Walpole and make sure they were safe. He'd known Bertha for a long time and would do anything for her.

As Bertha tucked into a meat pie and Walpole ate some fish, the girls asked Bertha about the tunnel she was hiding in. Bertha revealed that her father used to be a smuggler and he had created several tunnels as a secret way to travel around London without detection. Together with his cohorts, he had created quite a network of underground passageways that only they knew about – not even the police were aware of them.

There was one tunnel, however, that was so secret that no one else knew about – not even his gang. Bertha's father only told her about it on his death bed and she had promised that she wouldn't tell another soul about it unless it was an absolute emergency. Viola had asked for more details but Bertha stood firm. She wasn't going to break her father's trust. Her word was her bond.

As they listened to Bertha tell her father's stories of adventure, Viola realised that she was now strong enough to hear what she had to say.

"Bertha, we were wrong about Clancy. He's not the Governor."

Bertha turned to her, her mouth crammed full of pie. She raised an eyebrow inquisitively.

"B-who b-is b-it b-hen?" she tried to ask, spitting pie all over her lap. Viola looked nervously at Flo who nodded. It was time.

"It's Mr Collicott." Viola bit her lip and waited for Bertha to erupt with fury.

"Nay, Collicott's first name is Gus, it's doesn't fit the evidence," she said calmly, taking another big bite from the pie.

Flo sighed.

"He got the Book of Names from Plumb and he was the only person who knew about your money box. You said it yourself."

"Why else do you think he was so eager to see you behind bars? He didn't want to risk being exposed and thought you'd make a convincing substitute for Plumb," Viola added.

Bertha frowned. She still wasn't convinced.

"And Gus is short for Augustus."

Bertha stopped chewing and gasped, sucking in a huge chunk of pie. She coughed and spluttered and once she could breathe again,
she turned to the girls with shock etched on her face.

"Let's take him down."


Bertha had eventually fallen asleep in the den, surrounded by dogs and, of course, Walpole. Even though she was reeling from the discovery that Mr Collicott was the guilty party, she needed to rest in a warm bed. She was too exhausted to even take off her boots without help, let alone bring down a criminal mob.

Viola and Flo would go back to the clinic in the morning to meet her and come up with a plan to get Collicott behind bars once and for all.

As the girls returned to the bakery, Mrs Pumpernickel greeted them at the door.

"You two look very serious. What's happening?" she asked, wiping her hands on her apron. She was obviously cooking the dinner and it smelt wonderful.

"Nothing," Viola said, looking at Flo, who knew not to mention Bertha or the Governor.

Mrs Pumpernickel smiled and closed the door behind them. She was secretly relieved when she heard that Bertha had gone on the run. She was upset for Viola, of course, but felt that it was the best thing in the long run. The so-called Emerald Lady was a bad influence and she was happy she was out of their lives.

"Dinner will be ready in ten minutes. Take off your boots and go and wash your hands," she said, stroking her daughter's hair. Viola nodded and smiled back at her mother. "Oh, there's a letter for you, Viola. I left it on your bed," Mrs Pumpernickel suddenly remembered. Viola frowned; she never got post.

She rushed into the bedroom and scooped up the envelope from her pillow. She tore open the envelope and pulled out a tatty piece of paper and read it silently before passing it to Flo:

VIOLA,

THE BAKERY WILL BE ROBBED TONIGHT. I CANNOT SAY ANY MORE BUT PLEASE TRUST ME. WAIT THERE IN THE SHADOWS AND YOU WILL GET ALL THE ANSWERS YOU NEED. THE GOVERNOR KNOWS YOU ARE WATCHING – PLEASE BE CAREFUL.

FROM A FRIEND

Viola gasped.

"What shall we do?" Flo asked, worried. "Surely we must tell your parents?"

"No," said Viola firmly. "They won't believe us. This is our one chance to catch Collicott and Plumb – and we have to protect the bakery."

# Chapter Twenty-Three
### *The Fortress*

Brookwater Lane was eerily quiet. Viola and Flo sat behind a wall, several feet away from the bakery. Mr Pumpernickel had closed the shop hours ago and was relaxing upstairs with Mary and the boys, having had dinner. Viola had told them she was staying with Flo at her Aunt's for the night. She couldn't possibly tell them she was spending the evening trying to catch a thief and arsonist - and she most certainly couldn't tell them the bakery was the scene of the crime.

Their surveillance had taken an hour so far and they hadn't seen anything untoward. Well, they did see a man stumble out of the pub and try to start a conversation with a wall, but Viola recognised the man and knew he was of no harm to her.

The girls sat in absolute silence, staring at the bakery intently. They weren't going to make the same mistake as Bertha and fall asleep. No way.

The sound of footsteps drew their attention to Cobble Lane alley. A man appeared out of the shadows and quickly made his way over to the bakery, hiding under the hood of his coat. Viola grabbed Flo's arm and they sat in complete silence, nervously watching as he stopped by the door and stared through the window. He reached into his pocket and pulled out a long, silver stick. He glanced over his shoulder before pushing the stick through the keyhole and wriggling it. After a second or two, the door opened and he stood back, seemingly happy with his work. Viola scowled out of anger – how dare he try to hurt her family. Her fists clenched and her jaw tightened.

"Shall we stop him?" Flo whispered. Viola shook her head. They needed to catch him in the act of robbing the place so that Clancy had no choice but to accept what was happening. They couldn't risk getting this wrong.

As they watched, the man seemed to hesitate before going inside. He rocked from foot to foot, almost plucking up the courage to move. He lifted his shoulders and reached into his pocket, pulling out a rag and matchbook.

*He's going to set the bakery alight!*

Viola couldn't wait any longer. She ran towards the man and grabbed him, pulling him down to the floor. She sat on top of him as Flo grabbed his shoulders.

"You won't get away this time!" Viola cried.

"Get off me!" the man screamed.

"Digby?" Viola gasped. She pulled back the hood of his coat, seeing his face for the first time.

"At last! I was starting to worry you wouldn't get here in time," Digby struggled under the weight of the two girls pushing down on him.

"What do you mean?" Flo asked, confused.

"I sent you the note. I had to help you somehow and this was the only way to protect us all. I overheard Plumb and Crabtree talking and they finally said the Governor's name. It's that smug solicitor, Augustus Collicott,"

Digby explained that he had been trying to leave the Governor's gang for a while, but he never felt he was worthy of anything better. That was until Viola and Teddy helped Sonny. Then he realised that there were some good people in the world and felt he owed them everything. So, he decided to stay with the gang and learn all he could about the Governor so he could expose his devious plans.

"When I wrote you that note, I thought the bakery was the only job tonight, but I was wrong. I was sent here by Collicott as a distraction so that he and his men could focus on the *real* crime. This is all part of a diversion," Digby said quickly.

"Where is the real crime then?" Viola asked, concerned. Digby looked around before he spoke.

"All I heard him say was that it was happening in Threadneedle Street."

"Threadneedle Street?" Flo repeated. Digby nodded.

"The Old Lady - the Bank of England!" Viola gasped, suddenly realising what was happening. "The Governor is planning to rob the Bank of England tonight!"

"I'm worried that it's too late. It's on the other side of London, you'll never make it in time," Digby panicked.

"Oh yes we will," Bertha said, appearing behind them. "I think it's time you learnt about the Tunnel of Shadows."

Threadneedle Street was a seemingly endless road upon which many well-known buildings sat: the London Stock Exchange, the South Sea Company and the Berenberg Bank to name but a few. It was most famous, however, for being the home of the colossal Bank of England.

As he predicted, Collicott had been able to gain access to the bank with relative ease as his standing as an esteemed solicitor gave him a level of trust within those walls that very few people could muster. He simply arranged ahead of time with the Bank Manager, Mr Timms, that he would like to visit their establishment on behalf of a wealthy client to retrieve something valuable they kept in their safety deposit box held within the bank. Mr Timms had let him in and had provided him with the box to look through privately in his office.

Getting Plumb and Crabtree into the building proved far trickier, however. Neither of them looked like they had any business being inside a bank other than to rob it, and of course, that was their very intention so they needed a suitable disguise.

Collicott had told Mr Timms that Plumb was his security guard, due to the robberies happening in Brookwater Lane, and he felt uneasy roaming the streets alone. Mr Timms understood this and allowed Plumb to accompany Mr Collicott.

*One villainous sidekick in...one to go.*

Mr Timms left Collicott and Plumb alone in his office to peruse the deposit box, completely unaware of course, that Plumb would sneak out and hide in a nearby empty office until the bank was closed. Collicott told Mr Timms, upon his return, that Plumb had left to make sure the horse and carriage were ready for his departure. Mr Timms kindly escorted Collicott to the door and said his goodbyes, before locking up for the evening and going home.

Mr Timms was a sensible, intelligent man and knew that his job was a very important one. He also knew that some people wanted to have a lot of money without having to work for it and the easiest way, a lot of them thought, was to rob a bank. They never considered, however, just how difficult and dangerous that would be. You see, the Bank of England had never, ever been successfully robbed. Many people had tried and every single person had failed and all of them had ended up in jail for a very long time.

George Plumb, hiding under a desk in a pitch-black office, didn't know this of course. He believed that Collicott would be able to get them into the vaults, rob them of every single penny and walk out of the building as exceptionally rich men.

He waited for a good hour or so before making his move. He opened the office door to complete darkness. That was expected, as the bank was now closed. He crept slowly down the long corridor towards the staircase that Collicott told him led down to the vaults. What Collicott didn't tell him was that there was a burly security guard sitting at the bottom of the stairs reading a newspaper by candlelight.

As Plumb desperately tried to think of a way to pass him without being seen, Collicott and Crabtree stood outside the bank, waiting for Plumb's signal. He was supposed to have opened the back window by now to let them in so they could proceed to rob the place.

"He's late! Typical," Collicott snarled.

"I told you that I should have gone in. I'm far better at this sort of thing than 'im," Crabtree said, shaking his head.

"Oh, do shut up, Weston!  You're giving me a headache," Collicott hissed.

Plumb had been standing at the top of the stairs, looking down at the guard for twenty minutes. His brain was slowly whirring as he tried to think of another way down to the vaults.

*Collicott was right, I am an imbecile.*

Just then, the guard dropped the newspaper as his head fell to his chest. Within seconds, gentle snores bellowed out from the guard and Plumb's frown turned into a huge smile. He silently scurried down the steps, holding his breath as he carefully crept past the sleeping protector. As he did so, the guard let out a snort followed by a deep breath, but remained asleep. Plumb let out a silent sigh of relief and continued making his way down the long corridor. He eventually reached the window and peered through, seeing Collicott and his man outside. He twisted the lock on the sash window and pushed it open.

"About time!" Collicott boomed, before being shushed by Plumb. "Help us in."

"There's a guard just over there!" Plumb whispered. Collicott's eyes widened.

"Then you'd better help us in *quickly*," he spat, reaching his hand up.

Plumb helped his cohorts in through the small sash window and led them back to the staircase, repeating that the guard was close.

As they reached the foot of the stairs, Plumb looked over to the guard's chair. He gasped as he realised it was empty, save for the discarded newspaper.

"Uh-oh," Plumb whispered. "Where's the guard?" He frantically looked around using the light from Crabtree's lamp.

"We don't have time to search for him. Get moving," Collicott said, nudging Plumb forward. They raced down the long corridor towards the vault, Collicott's exhilaration growing with every step.

*My plan is working, I'm going to be rich - richer than my wildest dreams!*

As they reached the door to the vault, Collicott smiled. He was more excited than a child on Christmas Day. The vault's silver door was huge with a multi-pronged hatch in the centre. It was enough to render them silent with its sheer awesomeness. They knew it would be an impressive structure but this was just incredible. For just a second, the men stood in awe, staring at the one thing standing between them and a lifetime of untold wealth.

Snapping out of his daydream, Collicott removed his gloves and reached into his pocket. He pulled out a scrap of paper and read it quietly to himself. He crouched by the door and began turning the lock back and forth. He had managed to get the safe code from Mr Timms. He hadn't given it to him, of course, oh no, Mr Timms wasn't that silly. He had left it in a book in a cabinet in his office. Mr Collicott, being a nosey man, found it after a thorough search when Timms left him in the office unattended.

Having followed the code, he tried to unlock the door but it wouldn't budge. He sighed loudly and tried again.

Nothing.

"Are you sure you have the correct code, sir?" Crabtree asked. Collicott turned to glare at him.

"I'm the brains, you're the muscle," he hissed. Crabtree shrugged in response. As he twisted the lock one last time, the door clicked and popped open.

"My word, I'm good," he smiled, evidently happy at his own work. He took a deep breath and pulled the door open, his heart pounding.

As the door opened, the contents of the huge vault appeared through the darkness like an angel appearing from the heavens.

"Good grief, look at all that gold!" Collicott laughed. He had been dreaming about this robbery for years. It would be enough for him to retire and live very nicely for the rest of his life. In fact, it would be enough for several men to live off nicely for the rest of their lives. He had no intention of sharing his wealth, of course. Oh no. He'd live extravagantly and make sure he spent every last penny.

Crabtree and Plumb will go back to being paupers. Weasels like them were ten a penny - his brain, however, was priceless.

"It's - it's beautiful," Plumb laughed, his eyes starting to well up with joy.

"Me mother will be so 'appy!" Crabtree beamed. Collicott rolled his eyes and pushed Plumb into the vault. There were rows and rows of gold bars, stacked high, each one worth enough to live a very comfortable life indeed; a whole room full would provide more money than a man could possibly spend.

"There's so many - I don't know where to start!" Plumb laughed.

"Fill the bags with as much as you can. Hurry up!" Collicott said, following his men inside.

"Not so fast," came a voice from within the dark vault. Collicott froze.

"Who is it? Who's there?" he asked, taking a step backwards, completely thrown by the realisation there was someone already inside the vault. Viola stepped into the light of the lamp. Collicott's eyes narrowed. "You!" he boomed. "How on earth did you get in here?"

"You're a clever man, I'm sure you'll figure it out," Viola smiled, thinking about the Tunnel of Shadows. It was built by Bertha's father to run from Brookwater Lane to Kensington Gardens, passing directly underneath the bank's vaults. All they had to do was find the hatch that Mr Bard had put in place, many years ago.

"I've had just enough of you poking your nose into my business, Pumpernickel. If you don't leave right this instant..." Collicott growled. Viola took a step forward.

"It's over, Mr Collicott," she said, stepping forward. "Your plan might have worked had you predicted one of your men being a traitor."

"Who?" Collicott asked, fuming at their presence. "Plumb, I presume?"

"Oi!" Plumb yelled, outraged at the suggestion.

"Digby Travers. You thought you had him in your camp, didn't you, Collicott?" Flo laughed. "But he told us all about your little plan and he's currently on his way to the police station."

Realising he had been well and truly caught, he suddenly turned to run, however, Bertha and the security guard blocked his exit.

"Out of my way, gypsy!" Collicott boomed.

"You're not going anywhere, you rotten little worm." Bertha said. Collicott's cheeks reddened.

Desperate to help his boss, Plumb rushed to one of the rows of gold bars and pushed with all his might, causing the whole lot to topple over. The security guard raced to prevent them all crashing to the ground but he wasn't quick enough. The noise of hundreds of gold bars crashing to the floor was louder than anything Viola had heard before. The sound reverberated around the vast vault, seemingly endless in its assault.

"No!" The security guard cried as he rushed to the gold bars, somehow hoping he could stop them falling. In the commotion,

Bertha grabbed Flo and pulled her out of the way of a falling missile, dropping her oil lamp as she did so, plunging the vault into near darkness. Weston Crabtree found himself cornered by the fallen bars with nowhere to escape, letting out a cry of fear.

"Viola?" Flo yelled, desperately looking around the vault for her best friend. She turned to Bertha, rather concerned that she couldn't hear Viola respond.

"Mr Collicott, sir? Are you hurt?" Plumb cried, his voice trembling. He realised the extent of his actions and felt more than a little terrified of the prospect of angering his boss.

"Viola? Where are you, darling?" Bertha cried, searching behind her. As her eyes adjusted to being in the dark, she turned to the open door. "Collicott's taken her" she hissed.

"Stay here – keep an eye on them," Flo said to the security guard who nodded his agreement to keep Crabtree and Plumb in the vault until the police arrived. He would be more than happy to watch these villains get carted off to jail. Crabtree folded his arms across his chest and growled. He knew he wasn't going anywhere. Suddenly, Bertha lunged at him, grabbing him by the collar of his jacket.

"Where would Collicott have taken Viola?" Bertha asked.

"I ain't sayin' nothin'," Crabtree responded. Bertha squinted her eyes and glared at him fiercely.

"She's doing that mind reading thing, Weston. Close your thoughts!" Plumb cried.

"Close my thoughts? How do I do that?" Panic washed over him. He looked at Bertha and tried his best to think of something other than where he thought Collicott would be taking Viola.

"Plumb's cabin," Bertha said with a smile as Plumb let out a roar of frustration.

# Chapter Twenty-Four
## A Timely Plan

"Let me go!" Viola wriggled and kicked as Collicott carried her over his shoulder. He hadn't anticipated how strong she would be, and he was starting to regret grabbing her. He knew how fearless Viola Pumpernickel was. He should have realised that she would fight back.

"Stop kicking me!" he yelled, putting her down and grabbing her arm. "You will regret ever trying to outsmart me, Pumpernickel!" he hissed.

"Where are you taking me?" Viola asked, trying to pull free from his grip.

"You're a clever girl, you'll work it out," he laughed. Viola rolled her eyes at his mockery of her early comment.

He turned into Hyde Park and Viola knew instantly they were on their way to Plumb's cabin. He was going to keep her there until Bertha and Flo agreed not to go to the police. She could only imagine what he would do if they refused. Viola couldn't let that happen. She had to think up a plan of action.

As they walked past the treehouse, opposite the entrance to the tunnel Bertha was hiding in, Viola realised what she had to do. Collicott was too distracted with his own rage that he didn't notice Viola reaching into her apron pocket. She pulled out one of the bells that Bertha had dropped earlier and let it fall into the grass. She pulled out another one and dropped it a few feet away. She then scooped up a good handful of them and waited for the perfect time.

*Just a few steps more...*

Collicott led her past the industrial estate towards the cabin when Viola stopped suddenly, causing Collicott to twist round.

"Come on you little swine!" he growled. Knowing this was her only chance, she twisted his arm, kicked his shin and pushed him away. He fell backwards, shocked at her sudden outburst as she ran with all her might towards the old iron foundry, dropping the bells gradually towards the door like breadcrumbs in a fairy tale.

Running as fast as her legs would carry her, she burst through the door and into the disused factory. The interior was just as creepy as Viola remembered. Machinery stood abandoned, chairs were left on their sides, cobwebs covered almost every surface and the shadows played tricks on the mind; every shape looked demon-like in the gloom. She hadn't been inside this building for such a long time but it was still so familiar to her.

She could hear Collicott running behind her so she ducked behind an old machine and stopped. It was one of her usual hiding spots during games with her siblings. She could just about see him through a crack between the rusty machine and the wall. Collicott moved into the factory and stopped.

"Come out, come out, wherever you are..."

He took a step towards her hiding place as she froze to the spot.

*Please don't find me, please don't find me*

"I'm sorry if I scared you, little one. Please, come out and I will take you home to your mother and father," he sneered. Viola raised an eyebrow. She wasn't stupid, she knew it was a trap.

After a second or two, he turned and walked further into the factory. Viola let out a breath and looked over to the open door, leading to the woodland and ultimately, her freedom. Feeling sure he was a good distance away now, she slowly crept out from behind the machine and made a run for the door. As she did so, her dress caught on the side of a discarded metal device and pulled her back. She let out a cry of frustration as she tugged at the dress, desperately trying to free it.

Suddenly, out of the darkness, Collicott grabbed her arm.

"Gotcha!" he growled, pulling her towards an enormous machine that looked like it was used to melt hot iron. "You are going to regret ever sticking your nose into my business. I warned you. I told you to leave us alone but you couldn't resist!"

Viola's heart was thumping and her palms were sweating, despite the cool temperature of the old building. She frantically looked around for any way to escape but Collicott had her cornered.

*Somebody help me, please.*

"Aren't you afraid of the ghost?" Viola asked, stalling for time as she hatched a new plan.

"Ghost?" he asked, confused.

"The night watchman. He haunts the factory every night...he's terrifying."

"Nonsense," he laughed, swinging her round to get her closer to the huge machine, twisting her arm as he did so. "Nothing scares me!"

Suddenly a ginger cat leapt down from a balcony above them and landed on his shoulder.

*Walpole!*

"Aaarggghhh!" Collicott screamed, terrified at the creature that had appeared seemingly out of nowhere. "Get it off me!" he cried, spinning round and round.

Seizing her chance, Viola ran from him, disappearing into the dark shadows. Walpole, after digging his razor-sharp claws into Collicott's shoulder for good measure, launched himself off the villain and jumped onto a platform well out of Collicott's reach and appeared to smile, happy at his achievement.

"Get back here, Pumpernickel!" Collicott boomed, chasing after Viola.

He ran into the darkness which seemed to envelope him. He couldn't see further than his hand, save for the moonlight shining through a window. He walked slowly and carefully, desperate to find Viola. He was determined to make her pay for ruining his plans.

"You won't get away with this," Viola said through the

dimness. Collicott spun round, unable to work out where her voice was coming from.

"I already have, little girl," he snarled. "Nobody will find you here - your little team of detectives have no idea where you are. I'm going to turn you into soup!"

Viola, who by now had managed to climb up onto a second-floor balcony, could see Collicott and knew he had no idea that she was above him. She crouched down, making herself as small as possible and watched with glee as he stumbled about in the darkness trying to find her.

"I'll chop you into little pieces!" he yelled, grabbing what he thought was Viola, but realising it was just an old sack. Fuming with rage, he threw it on the floor.

"You'll have to find me first," she laughed, her voice ringing out around the empty building. He spun round, confused by the echoes and shadows.

Walpole trotted along the walkway to Viola and let out a meow when he met her. Viola shushed Walpole and gave his head a quick stroke, hoping to silence him. Walpole cried out again, flinging himself onto his back for a tummy rub. Viola tried to shoo him away but he wasn't going anywhere until his tummy was tickled. She looked down to the factory floor but couldn't see Collicott. She leaned forward, squinting her eyes to try and see clearer. She listened to the stillness of the factory, hoping to hear his footsteps.

*Silence.*

She stood and lent over the balcony, trying to find her adversary. As she looked into the gloom, Collicott appeared behind her. Walpole, sensing she was in immediate danger, let out a hiss and his hackles stood on end. Viola looked at him and shushed him again.

"You're going to get me caught, Walpole," she whispered.

"Too late," Collicott laughed as he threw his arms around her. She let out a scream, caught off guard by his actions.

"Let me go!" she cried, trying to wriggle free from his grip. Collicott, however, was determined not to let her escape again.

"It's over, Viola," he yelled, pulling her up by her apron and dangling her over the edge. She peered down, realising that if she were to fall – or be dropped – she would have a terribly long way to go before landing in the deadly melting machine.

"I'm sorry!" Viola said, her voice trembling. "Let me go – I'll tell everyone I made a mistake. I'll make sure you go free." She wriggled, desperately clinging on to the only thing she could reach – Collicott's arms.

*Please, someone help me. Grandfather, if you're listening, help me.*

"You have ruined everything!" Collicott was seething. "I planned for three long years and finally came up with the perfect plot to rob the untouchable Bank of England. Three years, and you come along and spoilt it all. You have to pay for that, Pumpernickel. Your time is up!"

As Collicott screamed the final four words at Viola, she knew what she had to do. She slowly reached into her apron pocket and wrapped the chain of her grandfather's pocket watch around her hand. In one slick move, she pulled the watch out of her pocket and swung it fiercely around her head, whacking Collicott on the nose. It caused him to cry out, instinctively letting go of Viola over the balcony. As she fell, plummeting towards the machine, she reached out and desperately grabbed a wooden plinth that jutted out, managing somehow to grip hold of it. The pain of holding her body weight on one arm was immense, but she knew she couldn't let go. She swung herself round and managed to reach out for a second balcony that ran alongside her, pulling herself safely onto it. She took a second to compose herself – every inch of her was shaking with fear. She looked at her hand and gulped. The watch had gone – she must have dropped it in the commotion. Her heart instantly filled with sadness it was all she had left of her grandfather.

She couldn't mourn her loss for long; Collicott was hot on her heels and she had to be quick. She sprinted with all her might to the staircase that ran along the back wall. As she reached the steps, she ran as fast as she could. Taking them two at a time, she raced up to the third level. Collicott was close behind, grabbing at her ankles. As she reached the edge of the balcony, she threw herself against the wall. Collicott grabbed her arm and pulled her close.

"You'll pay for this Pumpernickel! You're just a stupid little girl and you will never beat me! I am smarter than you, I will always win!" he boomed, trying to pull her to the edge. "You forget that I am the Governor. I am the most powerful man in London!"

Viola pulled with all her might, frantically trying to free her hand. She was fighting for her life now and there was no way she was going to lose.

She screamed as she finally yanked her hand free from his, throwing Collicott off balance. He stumbled backwards, falling off the gantry but landing on a platform slightly below it.

"And *you* forget that I know this place like the back of my hand," she smiled, suddenly pulling a lever that propelled him high into the air. Collicott screamed out in horror as the platform finally came to a halt, seven storeys above her. He wasn't as graceful in his ascent as Ruby Dancer was when she did it on the stage, I can tell you.

"Let me down!" he cried, the platform swaying. "You'll pay for this, Pumpernickel! I'll make sure of it!"

"Is that a threat, Collicott?" Clancy asked, appearing in the doorway of the foundry, with Flo and Bertha by his side.

"Constable Clancy!" Viola cried, racing down the steps to him. She instantly threw her arms around his chest, so thankful to see him there.

"Don't worry, Viola. It's over now," the policeman said, gently stroking her head.

"Thank heavens you're here, Clancy! This insane child has kidnapped me and is holding me against my will! She has some wild notion that I am a thief!" Collicott yelled from his perch high in the air.

"Stop all your bibble babble. No one believes ya," Bertha boomed, all her frustrations of the last few weeks coming out at once. "You tricked me into thinkin' you were me friend but you were just a sneaky skillimark. I'm glad I didn't trust you, Gus – I'd be in the cells for the rest of me life!"

"I have no idea what you're talking about. I-I was telling Miss Etheridge only this morning that I was a-a little hasty in my decision. Let me down and I will clear your name and help you find the real culprit." Collicott's voice was getting higher and higher.

"We already have the culprit, and he's up there on that platform," Flo laughed.

"You see, Mr Collicott, I knew you were somehow involved with the robberies when I came to your office," Viola explained. "I noticed your handwriting and realised that it was identical to that on the list we found in Plumb's cabin and on the address he dropped in the street. That seemed rather curious, but of course, it could have been just a coincidence. What we couldn't understand, however, was why you were so keen to see Bertha go to prison for these horrible crimes when you knew she was innocent? You must have been involved. Then, at the Wintertide Festival, you very publicly read from the Book of Names. The same Book of Names that Plumb had stolen from Bertha's home just a few hours earlier. How did you get hold of it if you weren't working with him? Another coincidence perhaps? Maybe. But then we realised that Gus was short for Augustus – and that your initials were A.C - the exact way the Governor signed his notes. Putting it all together, we were left in no doubt that *you* were the elusive Governor. Digby confirmed it when he kindly tipped us off to the robbery at the bakery and explained it was all a diversion. The real crime was to take place at the Bank of England. Bertha told us about a passageway that passed right underneath the vaults. We were there just moments before you arrived, ready and waiting for your bungled attempt to rob the place. Child's play, really," Viola smiled.

Collicott pursed his lips, anger seeping out of every inch of him. He was so angry, in fact, that it rendered him speechless.

"Why, Gus? Why did you want to cause such devastation to Brookwater Lane?" Bertha asked, crossing her arms across her chest.

"I am the most powerful man in London and without property, without ownership, I am nothing. I thought that if I destroyed the businesses, one by one, I could buy them cheap when their owners were down on their luck and desperate for money. Like your good friend, Mr Jeffers. He refused my offer of protection so I had to make him realise that you don't say no to Augustus Collicott. Once we were finished with him he would have sold that shop for an apple if I'd offered it! Road by road, street by street - one day I'll own all of London! Including your father's little bakery."

"I've heard enough, Collicott." Clancy yelled. "Get him down from there." Within seconds, at least ten policemen stormed the foundry and proceeded to get Collicott down and into handcuffs.

Bertha kissed Viola on the forehead.

"I think you dropped this," she smiled, handing her Edmund's pocket watch. Viola gasped as she held it close to her.

"This saved my life," Viola said quietly. As she held it close, she frowned. It was ticking!

"It seems that you had someone watching over you today." Bertha smiled. Viola closed her eyes and listened to the gentle *tick tock*, a sound she had missed dreadfully. Long forgotten, wonderful memories of her grandfather filled her head.

"We'll wait outside, Viola. Wouldn't want to get in the policeman's way," Bertha smiled before walking towards the door.

"Bertha?" Viola called, as she turned to face her. "Maybe magic does exist."

# Chapter Twenty-Five
*Just the beginning...*

A few weeks had passed since Viola stopped Collicott's gang and their roguish ways. Clancy had taken them to the station and they had been charged with stealing, kidnap, arson and fraud (it turned out that Collicott had been fleecing his most wealthy clients for many years) and were sentenced to five years hard labour in prison which, Viola found out, meant that amongst other things, they had to work on the docks, build roads and work down in the quarry. According to Mr Pumpernickel, it was "horrible work for horrible men." Clancy had apologised to Viola for not listening to her theories about the Governor and apologised for treating Bertha so badly. He knew she innocent but thought that if she was publicly arrested, the real criminal would let his guard down and somehow reveal his true identity. He also knew that Plumb was involved but he had no idea who his illusive leader was. He had tried to get Plumb to confess the evening that Viola saw them have the tussle in Brookwater Lane, but, as ever, Plumb remained blindly loyal to his boss.

As time went on, Viola's parents had understood the situation and now believed everything Viola told them. They had even invited Bertha to dinner a few times, which made Viola happier than anything else. Bertha didn't seem to have many friends, so it was nice to see her laughing with Viola's family.

Flo had returned to Brighton to spend Christmas with her Uncle James and Aunt Eliza. Albert had told Viola that the doctors had finally released Flo's mother from the hospital and that she was joining them at the house by the seaside as a surprise. Viola knew that would be the best Christmas present Flo could ever have.

"Viola?" Albert called from within the shop. "It's time for dinner. Come on, in you come." Viola turned from her spot on the step, as a beautiful song made her turn back to the street.

A small group of women were making their way down the street, singing the carol. The woman at the front held a candle and stopped now and again for people to throw a penny or two into a basket. The ladies glanced over at Viola and smiled. Their words gently rang out:

*"Away in a manger, no crib for his bed,*
*The little Lord Jesus lay down his sweet head.*
*The stars in the bright sky looked down where he lay,*
*The little Lord Jesus, asleep on the hay."*

Christmas was her most favourite time of year and even though they didn't have many presents, it was truly a magical time.

As the beautiful song rang out, Viola watched as Mr Jeffers hung a Christmas wreath on the door of his bookshop. It was still boarded up from the fire but knowing him as well as she did, she knew he'd still want it to look festive. He glanced over at Viola and waved at her with a smile. She smiled and waved back at the kind hearted old man, as a few flakes of snow started to fall from the sky. She held out her hand to feel the gentle fragments on her skin. Smiling, she turned her face up as the flakes grew heavier and faster. The choir moved slowly away from the shop, their enchanting voices echoing down the street as the snow fell:

> *"The cattle are lowing, the poor baby wakes,*
> *But little Lord Jesus, no crying he makes.*
> *I love thee, Lord Jesus, look down from the sky,*
> *And stay by the cradle 'til morning is nigh."*

Viola smiled and again, turned back into the bakery as Rupert appeared at the doorway. He looked up at his sister and smiled.

"Merry Christmas, Rupe," she smiled, rubbing his head.

"M-merry Christmas, Viola," he whispered in response. Viola's jaw dropped as she heard her brother's voice for the first time. She wrapped her arms around him and hugged him tightly. Her heart was fit to burst with happiness.

"Oi!" shouted a man from behind her, making her jump out of her skin. "Are you Viola Pumpernickel?" he said, appearing from the darkness. He was short and stout and Viola recognised him instantly.

"Who's asking?" Albert said, suddenly standing beside Viola and Rupert. He placed a protective arm across them.

"Walter Wiggins. I run Wilton's Music Hall down Whitechapel," he said, in between breaths. Viola nodded, she and Flo had seen him when they snuck into the theatre. She decided not to mention that to her father, however. He wouldn't be best pleased.

"I need your help, Viola. You solve crimes, after all, don't you?" he muttered, reaching into his pocket. "Ruby has gone missing."

"Ruby? Who's Ruby?" Albert asked.

"Ruby Dancer. She's our best girl at the music hall. She was going to be a star," he said, handing a piece of paper to Viola. "Here, read this. I found it in her dressing room not two hours ago."

Viola opened the paper to see a messy scrawl on the page:

We have your Ruby Dancer.

Pay us one thousand pounds and do not tell the police,

or you will never see her again. Our threat is real. Not a word.

The Black Tile Gang.

Viola gulped.

"I don't think this is really something Viola can help with…" Albert said, worryingly.

"I'll do it," Viola interjected. "I'll help you find her," she nodded.

Viola knew, in that very moment, that her life would never be the same again…

The End

Find out what happens next in:

# ViOla PumPerNicKel

## *and the*

## RubY DanCer

Printed in Great Britain
by Amazon